He hated living someone else's life.

He wasn't a laborer; he was a banker. Greg wasn't wealthy like the real Greg Bond, the man whose identity he'd stolen—borrowed. Alex Cooke was an upwardly mobile man with a wife and child.

He had to remind himself he no longer had a wife.

And Greg knew that just to get at him, whoever had killed his wife wouldn't hesitate to come after his daughter, too.

He had to remember his number one rule: stay as private as possible; don't involve others.

That included his daughter's pretty teacher, Lisa Jacoby.

Books by Pamela Tracy

Love Inspired Suspense   Love Inspired

Pursuit of Justice   *Daddy for Keeps*
The Price of Redemption
Broken Lullaby
Fugitive Family

PAMELA TRACY

lives in Arizona with a newly acquired husband (Yes, Pamela is somewhat a newlywed. You can be a newlywed for seven years. Ack, we're on year seven!), a confused cat (Hey, I had her all to myself for twenty years. Where'd this guy come from?) and a preschooler (newlymom is almost as fun as newlywed). She was raised in Omaha, Nebraska, and started writing at age twelve (a very bad teen romance featuring David Cassidy from The Partridge Family). Later, she honed her writing skills while earning a BA in Journalism at Texas Tech University in Lubbock, Texas (and wrote a very bad science fiction novel that didn't feature David Cassidy). Please visit her Web site at www.pamelakayetracy.com, or enjoy her blog at http://ladiesofsuspense.blogspot.com/ or write to her c/o Steeple Hill Books, 233 Broadway, Suite 1001, New York, NY 10279.

fugitive family

Pamela Tracy

Steeple
Hill®

Published by Steeple Hill Books™

STEEPLE HILL BOOKS

Steeple Hill®

ISBN-13: 978-0-373-44350-5

FUGITIVE FAMILY

www.SteepleHill.com

Printed in U.S.A.

Fear thou not; for I am with thee: be not dismayed; for I am thy God: I will strengthen thee; yea, I will help thee; yea, I will uphold thee with the right hand of my righteousness.

—*Isaiah* 41:10

To my father, Albert Hammonds Tracy,
who continually demonstrated that fatherhood
wasn't a job, it was a passion.

Also, as always, to the people who help along
the way to completion: my editors, my critique
group, my husband and son, and special thanks to
Roxanne Gould and Paige Dooley—
my final readers.

PROLOGUE

Six Months Ago

The bank teller flinched and tried to go faster. *Tried* being the operative word. She was going as fast as her shaking hands would allow. As she continued to stuff money into the old, blue backpack, he managed a quick look at the customers. Some were hunkered down on all fours. One big man in a wrinkled business suit sobbed louder than the pair of twentysomethings next to him. He never moved his face from between his legs. The twentysomethings did a strange hiccupy thing when they looked at the bleeding security guard. They stopped making any noise at all when they looked at him and his gun. Fear was a powerful motivator. Their forgotten paychecks and deposit slips lay on the floor beside their purses.

Funny how money became unimportant when faced with mortality.

He could see the frantic activity around him, feel the raw energy. He planned for the robbery to take six minutes. He knew the response time, and he knew the dangers of the get-away. Before entering the bank, he'd put an orange cone at the lot's entry. It wouldn't completely deter, but it might keep someone new from entering the bank *for at least six minutes.* Every detail had been perfectly planned, and in this moment, he felt a clarity he would never forget.

Without taking his eyes off the teller, he carefully pulled a pencil from his pocket, inserted it under his mask and scratched at a nonexistent itch. He intended to leave a pencil behind. Not the one he scratched with, but an identical one. One that had taken him three days to snatch; one that did not have his fingerprints on it, but someone else's.

He moaned in pretend relief. Then he lay the *other* pencil on the counter.

Ingenious.

He'd chosen the mask wisely, too. He wasn't wearing a boring black ski mask or impersonating some ex-president. Instead, he looked like a walking maggot infestation. The larvae had taken over his head, neck, and only those with very strong stomachs would wonder what was going on under his plain blue jacket. No one looked especially inclined to get too close.

He smiled. It was really too bad, because in actuality—this more than any other time—was his finest hour. And the critics would never know because this time he wasn't just acting, he was *being.* He didn't have props; he had tools of the trade. Real gun, real backpack, and in the parking lot a real getaway car. He glanced at the security guard. His blood looked real because it was real. The security guard was really the only victim here. The bank could spare the money. The bank manager deserved to spend his life behind bars. Unfortunately, the guard didn't deserve to forfeit his life. But first-offense bank robbers usually only got a slap on the hand, and this heist was designed to warrant so much more.

He hadn't expected to feel such a rush. But, then, this was his first time in the lead role, and obviously it was where he belonged. Soon, the world would recognize his talent.

And, really, his talent wasn't robbing banks.

He'd been planning this robbery for almost a year. There would be no mistakes and soon everything he wanted would be his. He knew this bank and its personnel inside and out. He knew that Wednesday was a slow day and that two major businesses made cash deposits right before noon.

He inched closer to the teller. He'd chosen her because not only was she the youngest, but she was also the new girl on the block.

"Faster, Helen," he urged. "Make it work."

She froze, fingers trembling, and slowly looked up. He grinned, not that she could see. He blinked a couple of times, hoping she'd notice the brown eyes.

She finished loading the money: all she had, all the tellers on either side of her had, all the money she could reach.

He grabbed the backpack. He turned, pushed aside a toddler and headed for the door.

He had the money.

He skidded to a stop just before reaching the door, turned one last time to survey the damage, and this time, he didn't just aim his finger for the pretend itch under his chin.

He put his whole hand there.

The mask popped off like a rocket. He frantically grabbed at it, holding it in front of his face, up, down, and to the side, all the while knowing he'd mastered the perfect look of surprise. Then, with the mask held just below his chin, he looked straight at the surveillance camera.

ONE

"I didn't kill my wife."

The voice, deep-pitched and steady, seemingly coming from nowhere, almost caused Greg Bond to drop his hammer. No one would have noticed. They were all busy. Wiping sweat from his brow, he forced himself to stay calm and listen for the sound of his own voice. It only took a moment to find the source, but the noise coming from the construction site drowned out whatever the radio news commentator might be saying next.

He located the radio. It took all Greg's will not to grab it, turn up the volume and listen to what the next chapter of his life might be.

He fell to his knees, ear pressed to the speaker, and listened as a monotone Paul Harvey wannabe managed four whole sentences.

"The body of Rachel Cooke was discovered earlier this morning in a deserted farmhouse in Yudan, Kansas. Her husband and the prime suspect, Alexander Cooke, already wanted for the murder of a security guard during a bank robbery last April, is still at large. The whereabouts of their six-year-old daughter, Amy Cooke, is unknown. Authorities believe she is still with her father and in danger. In other news…"

The radio commentator switched to the weather, as if the shocking discovery of someone's wife, mother, best friend, and a fifty-percent chance of rain deserved to be mentioned in the same breath. Greg's grip on his hammer loosened abruptly. The tool dropped to the ground. In all honesty, he'd forgotten that it was in his hand.

"Hey, Greg, you all right?"

Truth. Always stick as close to the truth as possible.

At one time he believed in telling the truth. He'd said it over and over to the authorities, to himself, to God. "I did not kill my wife. I did not rob the bank."

The truth didn't seem to make much of a difference then and it wouldn't work now, so he said, "I'm fine. Thought I heard the word *tornado*."

Greg picked up the hammer. Right now his heart was doing all the pounding he could handle. Funny, even after all these months, six to be exact, he'd still held out hope that Rachel was alive.

Never mind the blood. Never mind the words of his friends and neighbors. Personal opinion mattered little when compared to a video.

Vince Frenci, owner of the radio, shook his head and drawled, "Tornados knock things down—we build them back up. That's life. It's also job security."

But Greg knew life wasn't that easy. And security was fragile at best.

"I'm fine," Greg repeated, slipping the hammer into his belt and heading for his toolbox. Greg's coworkers called him a man of few words. Personal stuff didn't get bantered. He didn't socialize after work, and the few times wives had suggested "Hey, let's fix Greg up with…" he'd begged off.

They knew he had a daughter. They knew he'd moved to Nebraska a few months ago.

Gazing past the other five construction workers, their tools, their questioning looks, Greg focused first on the elementary school parking lot and then onto G Street. It would take him all of ten minutes to get to the truck and pick up Amber from the babysitter. What he had to decide was how to quit work without arousing suspicion, followed by an even tougher decision: whether it was time to disappear or time to take a stand. Or maybe he was right where he needed to be.

As if demanding a decision *now,* the vacuum that seemed to envelope him after hearing the news story suddenly ceased and the noise and hustle of "real" time returned.

"Yeah, everything's all right," Vince Frenci yelled to the owner of Konrad Construction, who no doubt had noticed Greg's momentary halt. "Greg just zoned out for a moment. I think he's checking out Mrs. Henry, the third-grade teacher. Hey, I was in her class twenty years ago. I still wake up crying."

"Maybe I'm not all right," Greg said, loud enough for Vince to hear. "I feel funny—maybe I'm dizzy. Maybe the sun's getting to me."

"Oh, dizzy?" Vince said. "Oh, la, la. Then, it's not Mrs. Henry. It must be that new first-grade teacher. She certainly made you light-headed yesterday. She makes me dizzy every time she gets outta her car. Better run down there, Greg, before she gets away."

Greg shook his head. They'd gone from teasing him about the seventyish gray-haired grandmother teacher to razzing him about the twentyish red-haired first-grade teacher. His daughter, Amber, would be in her class. Of course he was interested in her. All he'd done so far was introduce himself.

And, of course, his coworkers had noticed.

Yesterday, he'd almost enjoyed the attention. It made him feel almost normal. Now he was terrified. Normal wasn't allowed. Not until whoever had ruined his life was caught and behind bars. Today, he couldn't listen to his coworkers joke as if it were just another day, as if it were a world where everything and everyone looked and did just what they should. His world was no longer like theirs. They believed that when they left work for the day, they'd always have a home to go home to, a good woman waiting, security.

He'd believed that once, too.

The body of Rachel Cooke was discovered earlier today...

The site foreman squinted at Greg and hollered. "You're dizzy? Well, sit down before you fall down. We've got forty days without accident. I want forty more."

"I'm dizzy, too," Vince called.

"Yeah, but you were born that way," the foreman snapped.

Greg wavered. He checked out his coworkers. With the exception of Vince, they were all back to work. Sweat poured down their faces as it poured down his. Dirt edged around their collars, soaked into their knees and elbows, and found its way under their fingernails. This corner of the parking lot had caved in during recent rainstorms. Their job was to repair it before the first day of school.

None of them looked like they were thinking about the words on the radio.

It was all Greg could think about.

"You want someone to drive you home?" the foreman offered.

"I'll do it!" Vince volunteered.

Greg wasn't surprised. Vince probably knew more about construction than the rest of the crew combined. He certainly knew more than Greg, yet the man never missed an opportunity to find something else to do. He was the advice giver, the joke teller, the "just a minute" excuse maker. But when all was said and done, and know-how was needed, Vince was the man.

Greg packed his tools up and headed for his truck. "I can drive. It's just a headache and some dizziness."

"All right," the foreman said. "But call if something happens."

The mad urge to laugh caused Greg to duck his head as he

climbed behind the wheel. His boss's words echoed: *Call if something happens.* Something had *already* happened and every day it happened again and again in his thoughts, his memories, his dreams.

He needed to get home, turn on the television, log on to the Internet and call Burt Kelley. No, first he needed to get to his daughter, make sure she was safe, find out what she'd already heard.

Still, because it was expected, he promised, "I'll call if anything happens."

The foreman nodded, and Greg started his truck before his boss could say anything else.

Six months ago, a trip to the restroom had changed Greg's life forever. And no one on the construction crew knew how much. They couldn't know that just five minutes earlier Greg Bond, whose real name was Alexander Cooke, heard a truth he'd been both expecting and dreading for six months.

His wife was dead.

The authorities believed he'd killed her.

Some unknown entity had wiped out Greg's world and kept coming back for more.

Greg checked out the school's parking lot and put his foot on the gas.

It wasn't until he plowed into the passenger side of the first-grade teacher's car that he realized he hadn't been looking for traffic; he'd been looking for cops.

"Have I got the perfect guy for you!"

Those words, spoken barely an hour ago by one of her fellow teachers, didn't bode so well now. The perfect guy had just put a major dent in Lisa Jacoby's light blue Chevy Cavalier.

"I can't believe you hit me. Didn't you hear me honk?" Lisa

shook her head as she surveyed the damage. The front bumper was twisted and bit into the passenger-side tire. The fender had crumpled like cardboard. "The cops won't even come," she said, mournfully. "This is a private parking lot."

He looked at the street, first right, then left, and muttered, "I'm so sorry."

She'd been in fender benders before, and usually the people involved looked at each other or looked at the cars. Not Greg Bond—he seemed more concerned with the scenery.

"We need to call our insurance companies," she suggested.

It took him a moment, but he brought his attention back to her and this time he was the one to shake his head. "That's not going to work. I don't have car insurance."

"He's gorgeous, about thirty, single, his little girl will be in your class."

Gillian Magee, the teacher who thought Lisa needed a date, was more than right about Mr. Bond's looks. Definitely gorgeous, with shaggy black hair, he looked about thirty but hadn't mastered the clean shave yet. He wore a wedding ring, but everyone knew he was a single father.

He was everything Gillian had advertised. Lisa figured that out yesterday when he'd introduced himself.

"Oh, man. You've really done it now." Another construction worker joined them. His hair was black, too, but not shabby.

"Vince," Greg said, looking more distressed over his coworker's involvement than over his truck's attack on her vehicle. "We've got everything under control. Thanks for coming over, though."

"You really are dizzy? Man, I thought you were making it up. You plowed right into her." Vince bent down and looked under Lisa's bumper. "Too much damage to be hammered out and you're going to need a new tire and rim."

Greg winced before turning to Lisa and saying, "I've been meaning to get insurance. Look, you know who I am, and you have a whole construction crew full of witnesses. I'll get your car towed to a garage, and I'll pay for the damages. Every last dime. I promise."

Lisa knew what her sister, Tamara, the lawyer, would say. But, then, Tamara would detain the president of the United States if he didn't have proper insurance documentation. There were no gray areas in Tamara's world—only black and white. Her other sister, Sheila—the rebel—would simply blow the whole thing off. The car could be fixed; no one was hurt. End of story. Sheila was a writer. She'd incorporate the whole accident into a plot. Then she could even write it off on taxes.

Vince frowned. "Greg, you don't have insurance. Man, that's lame." He pulled a cell from his pocket and punched a number. "I'll call my brother. He works at a garage."

Lisa looked at Greg's truck. Not even a broken headlight. Soon she could hear Vince talking. His words were impressive enough. He correctly identified the make, model and year of her car. The assessment of damages sounded right. And, the words "Send a tow truck" were somewhat soothing.

Greg still studied the street.

"Am I keeping you from something?" Lisa asked, feeling annoyed. He'd hit her car, after all.

"Guess not," he finally muttered.

Vince grinned. "Greg's a little rusty when it comes to women. You're the new teacher. The guys were wondering why we didn't have any teachers who looked like you when we went to school here."

Lisa's cheeks flamed. She'd been in Sherman, Nebraska, all of two weeks. The first week had been spent finding a place to live. This week had been spent at Sherman Elementary School filling out paperwork, sitting through in-service meetings, and getting her classroom ready. She'd noticed the scrutiny from the construction crew, and while the other teachers laughed it off—most knew the men—Lisa'd wished the parking lot would return to normal: fast.

"How long before the tow truck gets here?" Greg asked, saving her.

"Instead of tow truck, I'll haul it over tonight. That will save you some money."

For the first time, Greg looked as if maybe the accident was something he *should* be concerned about. "How are you going to haul it?"

"I've got a hoist and a trailer at home. I'll—"

Before he could finish, someone shouted from the work site. Vince grinned sheepishly. "I gotta get back. Greg, you feel well enough to drive her home?"

He didn't wait for Greg to answer, but continued talking to Lisa, "Write down your address and phone number for me and leave a key."

It took Lisa a moment to retrieve her files from the passenger side of her damaged vehicle. When Greg's truck hit her car, folders had slid to the floor and the contents had spilled out. Finally she had her files together and climbed into his truck. He was still checking out the street and looked as welcoming as a grouchy pit bull.

"Are you expecting someone?" she said.

He closed her door and came around to get behind the wheel. He gave her a guarded look. "No, why?"

"You keep checking out the street."

He didn't answer.

"I live on Elm Street. Just past the library."

He paused, definitely torn about something, and then said,

"Do you mind if I pick up my daughter, Amber, from the babysitter first? It's on the way."

"Sure."

After five minutes of silence, she realized one thing for sure: Greg Bond wasn't into small talk. Usually, parents jumped right in, wanting to know what kind of a teacher she was, how many years' experience she had, if she volunteered time after school, and the like. Greg didn't ask a single question.

Even though she knew the answer, Lisa made an effort to bridge the silence. "How long have you lived in Sherman?"

"A little more than four months."

"Where'd you live before?"

He took his eyes off the road for a moment and studied her. He had blue eyes, stunning blue eyes, the color of cobalt. Not what she expected. Not with Indian black hair. She'd expected brooding dark-brown eyes.

"We moved around a lot. Not sure I'd call any place home. Where did you live before moving here?"

Okay, he changed the subject, from him to her, but at least she had a conversation going. "I'm from Tucson, Arizona. My family is still there."

"So what brought you to Sherman?" he asked. Not that he looked as if he cared to hear the answer. His attention was on everything but her.

"A bit of wanderlust. I graduated three months ago and didn't want to stay in Arizona. I wanted to travel, see the world. I have a good friend in Omaha, so I explored Nebraska a bit online to see where teachers were needed, and then applied here. The rest is history."

He didn't respond. Maybe he hadn't been listening.

"Like my car," she added.

He shook his head. "I deserved that. I do have something on my mind. Today's just not been a great day."

"Fine."

To her surprise, he didn't react to her sarcastic *fine*. He drove a few more blocks, pulled into a white clapboard house, and came around to open the door for her.

"You might as well come in. It always takes Amber some time to gather her things."

They'd only taken two steps toward the house when noise erupted from inside.

"That's my wild child," Greg said.

Something loud hit the screen door. Almost immediately came the sounds of "Daddy, Daddy, Daddy!"

"She sure gets excited when she sees you."

"Yeah," Greg admitted. "I hope that never changes."

It was the most human thing he'd said so far. But then, he'd stopped looking up and down the street and was focused completely on the scene in front of him. An elderly woman opened the door wide enough for Amber Bond to squeeze out and a bundle of energy, dressed in jeans and a blue T-shirt, launched through the air and into Greg's arms.

"Daddy!"

Lisa watched as relief relaxed his features. He hugged his daughter tightly and choked out, "Amber, did you have a good day?"

"Yes. Who's this?"

"This is your first-grade teacher. Daddy managed to hit her car with his car and she needs a ride home."

"You're my new teacher?"

"I am." Lisa bent down, eye level to the little girl, meeting a pair of blue eyes the same shade as Greg's, and said, "I'll bet you're six years old and that you are a good artist."

"How'd you know? Daddy! How'd she know?"

"Teachers have to be pretty smart."

Greg swung Amber up into his arms and held the front door open for Lisa. She followed him into a room where every surface screamed family. Photos dominated the walls. Lisa immediately got homesick. She'd gone two weeks without seeing her mother or sisters. She'd never been away from them before.

A gray-haired woman turned down the television and then offered Lisa her hand. "Since Greg seems to have forgotten his manners, I'm Lydia Griffin."

"Amber's babysitter and best friend," Greg added, putting Amber down. "Besides me, she's the only one allowed to pick Amber up from school."

"Overprotective father," Mrs. Griffin said.

Lisa figured that.

"Wise father," Greg countered.

"This is my new teacher," Amber announced before plopping to the floor to carefully load coloring books, lined notebooks, crayons, pencils and loose paper into a backpack. She had a place for everything and everything went into its place. "Daddy hit her car, and she already knows I'm a good drawer."

"Way to start the school year, Greg," Mrs. Griffin said before scrutinizing Lisa. "So you're the one taking over for Karen."

"Yes. She showed up at school today with her new baby. Everyone was excited," Lisa said.

"Daddy, look."

"We didn't think that girl would ever get married." Mrs. Griffin chuckled. "Then she met, married and quit working, all in a school year."

"A lot can happen in a short time," Lisa agreed.

"Daddy, look."

Finally, the grown-ups looked. The sound was off, but the

picture said it all: a bank robbery. The grainy surveillance camera caught the bank robber as he entered and exited. He wore a gray jumpsuit and some sort of mask.

"They're replaying that bank robbery from earlier this year," Mrs. Griffin said. "They found the wife's body. It's on all the channels."

"Daddy, look," Amber repeated. "You're on TV."

TWO

Amber's eyes remained glued to the television. Mrs. Griffin and Lisa turned to look at Greg. He wanted the floor to open up and swallow him whole. He absolutely did not know how to handle this.

Mrs. Griffin's look was one of amusement. She'd been watching Amber all summer and knew about his little girl's imagination. She'd seen the drawings Amber made of her friends, her cat and her history. History being what worried Greg. He suspected that Mrs. Griffin had a vague idea that somewhere, at some time, existed a mother with curly blond hair who liked going to the park, who liked to sit at a dinner table and eat pizza, and who liked to read books to a little girl who sat in her lap. He hoped Mrs. Griffin didn't question why sometimes the daddy in the pictures had brown hair instead of black, or why the little girl was blond. Mrs. Griffin probably knew Amber had lived in a two-story house, and it had been made of brick. She probably even suspected that Greg, judging by the cars Amber drew and the suit and tie Amber drew him in, had at one time worked in a white-collar job.

Lisa Jacoby had a look of pure curiosity. She knew little or nothing about Greg and Amber Bond, except what last year's kindergarten teacher, Gillian Magee, had managed to figure out during the last month of school—that the little girl drew all the time and that Greg was a bit of a hovering parent.

Truth. Always stick as close to the truth as possible.

Greg managed what he hoped was a straight face and said, "The bank robber is wearing what's called a grub mask. I bought one once, a long time ago, for a costume party."

"It scared me," Amber agreed.

"What exactly is a grub mask?" Mrs. Griffin asked.

"Maggot head," Amber answered.

"That's basically it," Greg agreed. "It's a mask designed to look like a maggot infestation. We no longer have the mask, and I'm sorry I taught my daughter the words *maggot head*." Greg gave Amber what he hoped was a stern look and then started to pick up her backpack. Instead, she scooted over and grabbed it. It was a continual power struggle of "I can do it, Daddy" versus "Honey, I'm not quite ready to let you take on the world."

Today, right now, he didn't care to battle. The most important thing was the fact that even though Mrs. Griffin had said the words, Amber didn't get that her mother's body had been found.

Didn't get that her mother was dead.

Didn't get that her father's heart was broken yet again and that there wasn't a thing he could do about it: not grieve, not scream, not even demand justice.

He didn't have the time or the energy. Not if he wanted to keep Amber safe.

"Are you all packed?" Greg asked quickly. He needed to get out of here before the ladies asked any questions, before the news ran a repeat of his denial and the sound of Alex's voice saying, "I did not kill my wife," made the ladies look at Greg.

And inspired Amber to say, "Listen, Daddy, I can hear you talking."

"Yes," Amber chirped. "I'm all packed."

"Thank you, Mrs. Griffin," he said, and hurried the ladies out to the truck, wishing he could simply pick Amber up and run—anything to get Lisa to her home and him to his—but no, Amber insisted on carrying her own backpack, dragging her feet, and casting curious looks at Lisa. Well, no wonder! It had been months since she'd seen a pretty woman—any woman for that matter—get into a vehicle with her father. He'd been so concerned about picking up Amber, making sure she was safe, that he'd forgotten his own rule.

Stay as private as possible; don't involve others.

He should have taken the teacher home first. Amber would have been fine. And this was just the beginning! Staying private had proved impossible from the moment he'd heard the news on the radio. Since the announcement, he'd been the center of attention of his coworkers—both in the parking lot and when he plowed into Lisa's car—and now, thanks to a grub mask, he'd also piqued both Mrs. Griffin's and Miss Jacoby's interest.

As Greg hoisted Amber into the truck, he whispered in her ear, "Everything's okay. We'll talk when we get home."

Amber nodded, scooted to the middle and started fiddling with the seat belt. Lisa reached over to help.

It was an everyday occurrence, a woman helping a child, but the sight of his little girl—short, black hair and Dora the Explorer shirt—and her teacher—shoulder-length, reddish-gold hair and dark blue dress—sitting side by side in the truck's cab and fiddling with the seat belts gave Greg pause.

Amber's mother should be sitting in the truck. She should be the one helping Amber with her seat belt, getting ready to send Amber off to first grade, and helping to raise Amber.

Lisa's hair was full and straight, instead of blond and curly, like Greg's late wife's. Lisa was about a decade younger. Lisa probably would live to a ripe old age, watching her children grow, and bouncing grandchildren on her knee.

His wife had made it to her thirty-third birthday. She'd given birth to one child, talked about a second. She'd never see her daughter graduate from high school, let alone get married and produce grandchildren.

Rachel Cooke's body had been discovered six months to the day after Alexander Cooke allegedly robbed his first bank and killed his first victim.

On the drive from the babysitter's place to the teacher's, Greg Bond didn't say a word. He gripped the steering wheel and stared, white-faced, straight ahead. He possessed a raw power she wasn't used to. Amber frowned at her father, confused, and then stared at Lisa with an expression of awe and fear. Finally, realizing that she had a captive audience, she opened her backpack.

"This is Tiffany." Amber put a drawing in Lisa's lap. "She's my best friend." It was a drawing of a pudgy girl with long hair in pigtails and wearing a yellow shirt and orange pants.

"I like her red hair."

"Me, too. I like yours."

Lisa glanced at Greg. He didn't glance back. Good, because it meant he kept his eyes on the road.

Amber didn't allow too much time for speculation. "Do you have a best friend?"

"I do, but she's back in Arizona. I have lots of good friends, though, who live in Nebraska, over in Omaha. Here in Sherman, I'm starting to make friends with your teacher from last year. Miss Magee."

"She's nice. This is Mikey." Another picture landed in Lisa's lap. "He's not nice."

"I take it this is Mikey Maxwell? From school?"

"Yes, and he's mean."

For the rest of the drive, Amber pretty much introduced Lisa to all the students who'd be showing up in the first-grade classroom on Monday. Lisa managed to convince Amber that names were enough because Amber was clearly willing to divide Lisa's future students into two categories—mean and nice.

By the time Lisa made it to her apartment, she was in the mood to buy colored pencils and a drawing tablet. She cheerfully accepted a hug from Amber and then said goodbye to Greg, who barely waved as he put his foot on the gas.

Since it hadn't been a date, Lisa didn't know why she was so annoyed at the way Greg had dropped her off. He didn't see her to the door; he didn't idle by the curb until she got inside.

Her sister Sheila was right. Men who acted uninterested were the most interesting men of all.

She was intrigued as she climbed the stairs to her attic apartment. It really was too cute for words, *as was Greg Bond*. In her native Tucson, Arizona, Lisa had never even seen an attic apartment. The attic in her childhood home had been a crawl space where her father stored Christmas decorations. None of her friends' homes had boasted real attics or basements.

Nebraska had plenty of both.

Her landlady, Deborah Hawn, rented the basement apartment to a computer geek. He had shaggy hair and apparently seldom ventured out. Lisa had only seen him once. Her place—A-shaped and long, with a living room in the middle, a bedroom at one side, and the kitchen and restroom at the other—was a perfect starter home.

It came furnished. She'd only needed to buy bedding and a few odds and ends. What really sold her on the place, though, was the tiny balcony. Just big enough for a rocking chair and a little table; she could sit outside in the early evening and watch the park next to the library. There was always something going on.

Like tonight.

Lisa made herself a peanut butter and jelly sandwich, poured a glass of milk and sat down outside. Whoever said it didn't get hot in Nebraska had never been to Nebraska. She leaned her head back, closed her eyes and relaxed.

Maybe this time next year, she'd be on one of the softball teams, practicing in the park in front of her. She'd played second base in high school. Or even better, maybe in a few years she'd be chasing a toddler, and instead of living in an attic apartment she'd be living in one of the Victorians just a short way from downtown.

The evening light was fading when she finally went inside and sat down to finish the work she'd brought home. She worked on smoothing the wrinkles. In the middle of working, she came across Greg's phone number. He had straight up and down block handwriting, no cursive, and he used a clear stroke.

She'd gone through four years of college, dated more than her share, nothing even close to serious, and none of the guys had her studying their handwriting. What was it that drew her to him? This quickly and with no reason? So far, their two encounters had to do with an overeager father and a fender bender.

Was it the exuberant way his daughter greeted him? Amber's eyes lit up and it was as if someone had switched on the light to her whole world.

He was also the type of man who called his babysitter by her proper name instead of her first name.

Her final thought before she drifted off to sleep was that she'd almost think of him as a gentleman, if only he'd walked her to her door.

Thursday morning, Lisa's eyes opened at six. In the hazy

morning sunrise, she stretched, looked in the mirror and quickly realized that, without a car, she wasn't going to be driving to work.

She'd been a little remiss in getting all the phone numbers she needed yesterday. And last names, for that matter. She knew Greg's information, but all she had for Vince was a first name, and it was really his brother who had her vehicle.

A quick call to Gillian garnered a ride to work, a quick shower solved the morning's doldrums and a quick breakfast filled her stomach.

By seven she was outside and waiting for Gillian.

No doubt Gillian, who knew everybody and everything, would not only know Vince's last name, but also what year he'd gone to high school, where he lived, whom he loved and where he went to church.

Church seemed like a staple of the Sherman community. Gillian had been more than surprised when Lisa not only turned down the invitation to church, but also admitted to not attending at all.

"What do you do when you're lonely?" Gillian had asked.

Lisa didn't have an answer. Until moving to Sherman, she had never felt lonely.

"Daddy, you're on TV again!"

Greg looked up from the Internet. Since last night, and really all through the night, he'd read a hundred different reports on the discovery of his wife's body. He'd watched a dozen videos. Yudan, Kansas, was a farm community of maybe two thousand souls—most quite wealthy. Still, as in most areas, there were pockets of poverty. A broken-down mobile home, a century-old unpainted barn, a few falling-down, deserted farmhouses.

Rachel's body had been discovered by kids thinking that a

deserted farm was the perfect place for a party. They'd been wrong. Oddly enough, the cops acknowledged that the farm was a common party destination and that the kids hadn't stumbled upon the body because, until this particular party, the room had been locked.

The cops were pretty sure that more than twenty kids had trampled over the crime scene. Fifteen didn't stick around to wait for the cops to arrive after an honors student with a conscience used her cell phone to call her mother.

Right now, cops were still working on the five teenagers who'd stuck around to face the music. They all had the same story. The room was always locked. No, they hadn't noticed an odor or anything out of place. They had never seen any strange adults or cars near the place.

The nearest neighbor, and the owner of the farm, had purchased the property ten years ago, meaning to do something with it, and simply hadn't got around to it. He didn't know the teenagers were breaking and entering.

Greg had never been to Yudan. Until her death, he doubted that his wife had, either, even though it was only ninety miles from where they lived. Cops weren't saying if she died before or after she'd arrived at the farmhouse.

They probably didn't know yet.

One thing the cops did know, according to the news, was that Rachel Cooke's husband, Alex Cooke, still on the run and suspected of snatching his then five-year-old daughter, remained the key suspect. The cops weren't commenting on one item that the five teenagers had reported.

There were flowers in the room Rachel had been found in. Lots of flowers. Some dead and brittle. Some wilted and sad. And one bunch amazingly fresh.

Like the cops, Greg had his own suspicions. The cops

thought Alex Cooke had been bringing flowers to his wife and had forgotten to lock the door.

Greg knew the key suspect was the same person who'd robbed the bank in Wellington, Kansas—*his bank, the one he'd managed.*

Greg also knew that the murderer was someone both he and Rachel knew. Because the flowers were the kind they'd used in their wedding. Rachel's favorite: daisies.

"Daddy, come look. It's you again!"

It wasn't. The morning news simply highlighted a maggot head who six months ago had made it his business to look like Greg, like how Greg looked when he could go throughout his day as Alexander Cooke. Luckily, it was easier to change the channel than it had been for him to change their lives.

Greg took another drink of lukewarm coffee as he left his office and headed to the living room to settle down next to his daughter. He was amazed at the curve life had tossed him. Still, he knew how to play ball. It was what the curve had done to Amber that really got to him. She'd just started sleeping through the night, making friends and letting go of his hand.

Nonchalantly, he changed the channel on the television, moved closer to Amber and took her in his lap. His little girl had a best friend, two if he counted little Mikey Maxwell. She was sleeping through the night. She was actually looking forward to school starting. She was recovering, somewhat.

He wasn't.

Together they watched an early-morning kids program. When it ended, Greg said gently, "Honey, remember, the man you saw on the news in the maggot mask is not me."

Amber slowly nodded. "I know. It's a man pretending to be you." She scooted into his arms and he felt the warmth of her body, the beating of her heart. Six years old was too young to deal with everything she had to deal with. Unfortunately, six years old was also old enough to do things on her own. Like turn on the television when he'd specifically told her not to. Still, he didn't have it in his heart to punish her.

"Daddy will take care of this," he promised. "The only thing you have to do is not tell anybody our real names or about our old life. Not until Daddy figures out what's happening."

She nodded, or at least, he felt her head go up and down.

Six months ago his daughter had been full of energy, her cheeks were rosy, her smiles contagious. If she turned pale, serious, or vulnerable, her mommy was right there to lay a gentle hand on Amber's forehead, to tickle the seriousness away or to scoop her up and shelter her.

Six months ago he'd been the assistant manager at a bank in Wellington, Kansas. Then, at least according to the police and everyone who listened to and believed the five o'clock news, he'd not only robbed his own bank, but he'd also shot and killed the security guard. Then, apparently, by accident, his mask had come off, and he'd looked right at the security camera.

Right.

The news commentators had a field day with the irony of a bank manager who had to know where the camera was, looking right at the lens.

The Dr. Phils of the world had had a field day with the kind of criminal mind that aimed a full smile at the security camera.

Right.

He'd been stuck in the restroom during the whole robbery. He hadn't even known what was going on until he'd somehow managed to push open the door.

No one believed him.

"Today we're staying home," he told Amber. "Daddy has to keep track of the news."

"Will we move again?"

"I'm not sure."

"Will I have to go to another school?"

"Not sure about that, either."

"I don't like moving."

"I don't like moving, either."

Unfortunately, moving was on a long list of don't likes. He didn't like living on the run, he didn't like construction work and he didn't like that whenever he called, he got Burt Kelley's answering machine. With all that was going on, you'd think the only person on his side would make himself available.

He needed to try Burt again. He needed to find out what was happening behind the scenes. Needed to find out what had really happened to his wife.

Needed to find out if she'd been dead for six months, as the bloodstains on the living room carpet of their Wellington home implied. Or if she'd died more recently, which meant that while the authorities spun their wheels blaming him, they could have spent their time finding Rachel and *maybe saving her.*

THREE

She looked for Greg on Thursday, but he'd called in sick. No surprise. He, or maybe it had been the Vince guy, had mentioned a dizzy spell.

It was Vince whom Lisa saw first. Watching him meander through the elementary school hallway was enlightening. He bumped into Mrs. Henry by the cafeteria and ducked his head like a bashful schoolboy. Then he made a brief foray into the library, before finally heading for Lisa's classroom to hand her his brother's business card.

Just before noon, and her first break from a too long meeting, he'd come in with a status report. He settled himself in a first-grade desk—not an easy task—and folded his hands like a good boy. She doubted that he realized just how dirty his hands were. His brother, he reported, didn't have the right fender but could find one in a few days. His brother did, however, stock the right make and shade of paint.

The tire had already been replaced.

Oh, and she was looking at just over $2,000 in damages.

The third time Vince showed up in her classroom, he'd offered her a ride home.

Luckily, Gillian—who'd already promised Lisa a ride home—arrived in the classroom a moment later, sat down at the small desk next to Vince and promptly began a three-way conversation that Lisa never would have instigated. She started with, "Does Greg Bond ever date?"

Vince grinned, his eyes crinkled, and with a cocky expression that said he wasn't surprised by the question, replied, "Gillian, you're still as nosey as you were when we were both in first grade. I think you sat in the front row back then, too."

"And you," Gillian said, "are still just as annoying and belong in the back row. Now, does Greg Bond ever date?"

"Not that I know of. He doesn't even talk about chicks—" He stuck his tongue out at Gillian and then looked at Lisa with what had to be a pretend-sheepish expression. "I mean *women.*"

"He still wears his wedding ring," Gillian pointed out.

"We've told him to take it off," Vince sobered. "It's dangerous on the job. I've heard of men losing fingers because of wedding rings."

"He never talks about his wife."

Vince nodded. "She had to have been young. All he says is that she died in an accident."

Lisa thought back to Amber's school records. The only thing she'd seen relating to Amber's mother was the word *deceased.*

"He goes to my church," Gillian said. "Amber's in my Sunday morning Bible school class. She never misses a class. They attend both services—on Sunday and Wednesday night. He's never asked for prayers, never engaged in small talk. He plays on the church's softball team, but I think the preacher strong-armed him. I think he's sad."

"I think he's sad that he hit Lisa's car," Vince agreed.

Lisa thought back to the man who'd just last night insisted on getting his daughter before going home, who so solemnly watched as they buckled up their seat belts, and who gripped the steering wheel as if it were a weapon.

Sad wasn't the word she'd use to describe him. At first she'd thought *distracted* and maybe a bit *unfriendly,* but now she realized that Greg Bond looked haunted.

Burt Kelley finally called Thursday night. Greg made sure Amber was busy drawing at the kitchen table and went into his office. Burt didn't have good news. "The footage you're seeing on television leaves out a few key issues."

"Such as?" Greg asked.

"I can tell you the definites, the ones you'll see on the news tomorrow. The flowers the kids reported were also tied with red ribbon, like they were at your wedding. They found shoe prints on the floor of the bedroom that are the same size you wear. Those two items are the most damning. Still, they didn't find fingerprints on the ribbon and a lot of men wear size 12 shoes, including me."

"You also know the colors Rachel picked out for the wedding."

Greg could almost picture Burt. Back in high school, Burt had been one of Greg's many friends. Today Burt was his only friend. Slight and pale, Burt didn't look impressive, but he had the heart of a gladiator.

Burt continued, "The farmhouse has been used as a party place before, many times. If there was any evidence outside the room Rachel was found in, it's been irrevocably compromised. The bedroom where the two teens found Rachel isn't as compromised."

"They won't find anything that leads to me!"

"Don't be cocky," Burt said snidely. The remark took Greg all the way back to junior high. He and Burt sitting behind the school, smoking cigarettes and looking for trouble. Burt always found it. Until six months ago, Greg had always managed to sidestep it.

Just his luck the first time trouble landed in his lap, it was for something he didn't do, something he had no control over.

"Well, what should I be worrying about? What won't they be releasing to the media tomorrow?" Greg asked. "Did I leave another pencil at the scene? Or maybe I left a Polaroid, or even better, I videotaped the murder and just happened to leave the tape behind."

"Don't say that—not even to me."

While Greg had gone to college, Burt had gone to jail. He'd been straddling the three-strikes-and-you're-out law when a Texas judge challenged him.

Get a life or serve life.

Burt figured he was only good at one thing: being a criminal. He turned that gift into a career of catching criminals. Right now, Burt was a fairly well-known and successful bail enforcement agent—a bounty hunter—who currently worked for only one client.

Alex Cooke.

He was the only person, besides Amber, who knew that Alex Cooke and Greg Bond were one and the same.

"Okay," Greg agreed. "I won't say it again. But I'd still like to know what it is they think they have that ties me to Rachel's murder."

"Believe me, I intend to find out," Burt promised. "Greg, I've investigated every employee you've worked with, and some who came before and after. I've tracked down people who blamed the bank for loans gone bad, people who were denied loans and even John Q. Public, who is plugging along paying off his loan. I've dug into the history of the contract workers the bank has hired. I know about the people who clean the bank, the men who take care of the grounds, and all the delivery people.

"I've spent the last twenty-four hours trying to see if any of the people I've investigated in the last year can be tied to the Yudan area. I've looked into who owns all the land within a hundred miles. I've checked family histories. And I've come up with nothing. I think it's time to stop focusing on you, on who has a vendetta against you. In truth, you were a workaholic who really didn't get out much. Based on the killer's dedication to bringing flowers to Rachel's burial site, I think it's time to look closer at your wife's history."

"Everyone loved Rachel."

"And that might very well be the motivator. I've already started some preliminary investigating. Rachel was very social. Look, Greg, I'm calling you from a hotel near your old house. I've already visited the gym she belonged to. I'm starting my list of who she said hi to and who worked out in the morning at the same time. I've been to the grocery store where she bought food, her favorite clothing stores, toy stores and bookstores. I know her favorite coffee shop, lunch place and everyone who ever had a playdate with Amy. I've even—"

"Enough," Greg said. "Investigating my life and my wife's life together seems to have gotten us nowhere. There must be another angle."

"I want to go back further. On both of you."

Greg could only shake his head. "I don't even remember all the foster homes."

"Well, navigating the foster-care system happens to be a skill of mine, and since we shared an address or two while in the system, investigating your youth shouldn't be so hard," Burt said. "I'm going back further on your wife, too."

Greg shook his head, not that Burt could see. "Good luck. She was the darling of Lawrence, Kansas. Cheerleader, class vice president, lead in her senior play."

"And she married you? What *waaas* she thinking?"

Before Rachel's death, the comment would have garnered a chuckle between two friends who'd somehow managed to make good. Today, it only reduced them to a silence that Burt finally broke.

"How often did you visit her hometown?"

"Since her family died, not very often. It made her too sad. I think in the last five years the only trip we made to Lawrence was for her high school reunion."

"Her family have money I don't know about?" Burt asked.

"No, everything is upfront. Her dad owned a hardware store. Mom was a homemaker. What do you think?"

"I think they didn't have money."

"I made more money in a week than her dad did in a month," Greg said. "Which is another reason why it makes no sense to portray me as a bank robber. My robbing a bank makes about as much sense as me killing my wife. Why would I kill her? Why? I loved my wife."

"The world seldom makes sense," Burt said.

He'd said the same thing all those years ago when they were taken from a "good" foster home, not given a reason and placed in another.

Silence returned.

Finally, Burt said, "The best news I can give you is that nothing ties Yudan, Kansas, to Sherman, Nebraska. You're safe for the moment. Stay put, act normal and thank God."

Greg closed his eyes, feeling choked up. A year ago, if someone had told him to thank God, he'd have laughed. God was for the weak. Greg, as Alex, had been too busy carving out a life to spend time *with* and *for* God.

A stolen identity, a scared child, and a black void in his life had somehow landed him in God's capable hands, and if it weren't for the Bible and the church, he'd be lost, so lost, when it came to raising Amber without her mother.

When Greg could talk again, he said, "I'm not turning myself in. More than anything, I want to be involved in the investigation. I want to answer their questions and work alongside the authorities. But every single newscast has declared me guilty. What about innocent until proven guilty? Burt, during the time it would take to clear me, Amber would be in foster care. I won't allow that."

"I, more than anyone, understand. And if I wasn't already a person of interest—they've stopped me for questioning twice— I'd take her. Greg, man, you have to find someone you trust. Someone who will disappear with Amber until you clear yourself and we find the real culprit."

"There is no one. Give me another suggestion," Greg said, gritting his teeth. Burt knew there was no one to leave Amber with, but he kept asking. Greg and Burt both had been raised in the foster-care system, which is why he'd do anything, be anything, to keep Amber out of it. Rachel's parents and younger brother had died in an automobile accident when Rachel was a freshman in college. And it wouldn't be fair to ask a church friend to watch Amber, because all it would do is pull one more soul into this wretched game.

Besides, he couldn't imagine any of the good souls at Sherman's Main Street Church willing to disappear, to run, should the need arise. Amber's safety was up to him. Now it was Greg and Amber and God against the world.

"Okay, stay in Nebraska," Burt relented. "But, remember, go out in the evenings. The more people who see you the better. Somehow our killer's going to stumble, and I want you to have alibis for every minute of the day. Remember, act normal."

Greg hung up the phone and stared at it for a few minutes

before going to check on Amber. *Act normal.* Rachel was the actor in the family. It wasn't fair that Greg had the job now.

The last thing Greg wanted to do on Friday was return to work. He really wanted to stay glued to the Internet, typing in keywords, and looking for newly released footage. But he knew Burt was right about being seen in public. The discovery of Rachel's body meant the FBI was back to making Alexander Cooke a top priority—again. They'd be looking for *him*.

Only three people knew that Alexander Cooke had dyed his brown hair black, started wearing blue contacts to hide brown eyes, worked with tools instead of numbers and drove a Ford truck instead of a BMW. Alex, aka Greg Bond; Amber, whose real name was Amy; and Burt.

Act normal. There was nothing normal about living under an assumed name, dying your hair and your daughter's hair every few weeks, and jumping at shadows. But Greg had done it for months now. If it kept Amber safe, he'd do it for the rest of his life.

"Hey, Greg!" Vince pulled up next to him in the elementary school parking lot. "Surprised you're back. Dizziness gone?"

"Yes."

Unfortunately, short answers had never deterred Vince.

"I spoke with my brother yesterday. You did over $2,000 in damage to Lisa's car. She doesn't seem too mad. Her and Gillian sure had a lot of questions about you."

For a moment, fear threatened to spill over. The urge to run surfaced. Greg reined in both emotions. "What kind of questions?"

"What do you do for fun? What happened to your wife? Why you're still wearing your wedding ring."

The typical questions single women always asked. Keeping

the wedding ring was probably a mistake. It was the ring Rachel had slipped on his finger nine years ago. It was the only visible link to his past. He'd taken it off right after he'd snatched Amy from her friend Molly Turner's house. He'd put it back on a month later. Sometimes he felt it was all he had left of Rachel.

"Why do you think she had all those questions?" Greg asked, although he knew. He was a single man in a town of single women.

"It wasn't Lisa so much—more Gillian. Let me tell you, she talked her way through school the first time and, boy, she's still talking."

Amber's former kindergarten teacher was outgoing. Greg had two-stepped around many a question during the last month of school. Then, wouldn't you know it, when he decided to try his neighborhood church—something to do and a way to get Amber socializing—there was Gillian, introducing him to people he didn't want to meet and asking even more questions he couldn't really answer.

Thank goodness Gillian was engaged. It meant she wasn't looking at him as a potential suitor. Unfortunately, Greg knew the fiancé, even played ball with the man, and didn't much care for him. Maybe because Perry Jenson reminded Greg too much of ol' Alexander Cooke, climbing the corporate ladder and spending more time at work than with the people who loved him.

Greg followed Vince to the job trailer. It only took a few minutes to get his assignment and then he was doing cleanup. It took Vince another half hour before he joined Greg, turned on his radio and began life as usual. Where Vince had been for thirty minutes, Greg didn't want to know.

Vince put on his gloves and looked at Greg. He started the conversation right where they had left off. "I told them you needed to take off your wedding ring because it's dangerous to wear. I told them that you don't socialize much. Really, Gillian seemed to know more about you than I do."

Greg had been paired up with Vince plenty of times. Vince knew that last year Miss Magee had been Amber's teacher. You'd think he'd have mentioned knowing her.

When Greg didn't respond, Vince said, "Gillian happened to be there when I stopped by to tell Lisa about my brother's estimate."

"The one that's going to cost me an arm and a leg."

Vince nodded. "That one."

"What did Miss Jacoby say?" Greg had a hard time keeping his mind on cleaning up. Today he and Vince were the only ones doing all the odds and ends that came with completing a job. The work was virtually done. Almost everyone else had been sent other places.

"Lisa didn't say nothing. Until my brother gets the fender, there's nothing to say. She's been bumming rides with Gillian."

As if beckoned by Vince's words, Gillian pulled into the parking lot. Both men stopped, walked to the edge, and watched. Gillian moved quickly. She was out of the car and un-loading stuff from her backseat before Lisa had the passenger-side door opened. Both women wore those jeans that didn't quite reach their ankles. Lisa also had a pink short-sleeved shirt, and her red hair was in a ponytail, reminding Greg how young she was.

"Yowza," Vince said.

Greg could only nod. School started on Monday and all the teachers and staff were arriving. A typical day, *for them.* He needed to do the right thing and take care of her car. After all, he might not be here in another twenty-four hours, depending on what Burt found out.

He hated not knowing the future. Hated living someone

else's life. He wasn't a laborer; he was a banker. Greg wasn't wealthy, like the real Greg Bond, the man whose identity he'd stolen—well, borrowed. Alex Cooke was an upwardly mobile young man with a wife and child.

He had to remind himself that he no longer had a wife.

Vince's radio, newly turned on and blaring before the start of the morning duties, reiterated that fact.

Authorities had just determined that the gun used in the bank robbery—the gun that killed the security guard—was the same gun used approximately six months ago to kill Rachel Cooke.

FOUR

Since she didn't have a ladder, Lisa used one of the children's desks to help her get to the out-of-reach places where she wanted to put "Welcome Back" posters.

Right before lunch, Vince meandered in. Greg, looking as if he'd rather be anyplace but here, and as if he hadn't slept a wink, was right behind him.

Haunted. Yup. Distracted, too, but not unfriendly.

Vince didn't waste any time. "My brother says it's going to be a few days before you get your car back."

It was rather fun to gaze down at them. Vince looked like he'd willingly catch her if she fell. Greg looked like he expected her to fall *and break*. She put him out of his misery, climbed down and said, "I like riding with Miss Magee. It's not a problem. *Really*," she emphasized looking right at Greg and smiling. "There's no need to feel bad. Are you all right?"

"He woke up grouchy," Vince said. "Me, I woke up just fine, and I can give you a ride anywhere you need to go this weekend, too. My brother says he'll have the fender tomorrow, and your car should be ready Monday at the latest."

"If possible," Greg said, tersely. "I'll head over there Monday and check out the car with you. Then, after you look at it and are sure you're happy, I'll pay for everything. We'll make it work."

Then, before she could ask questions, they were gone. Well, at least Greg was. Vince hung around a moment talking about dinner, movies, playing pool.

Lisa checked her watch and said she was meeting someone.

That someone was Gillian, who five hours later, gave Lisa a ride to the old Victorian that Lisa called home. Just after six, fading daylight offered the first hint of evening shadows. The wind sent a few leaves blowing up the sidewalk. Lisa opened the car door and started to step out.

"The folks playing softball across the street are the team from my church," Gillian said. "They're excited. Tonight's their first game in this final season. I'm going over to watch. Why don't you come along?"

Lisa glanced at the park. She'd watched so many of their practices from her balcony that she almost felt as if she knew them. They had a strong first basewoman and pitcher. The outfield was okay, but second and third base were clearly the weak links. It would be nice to put names to the players. They'd be around for Lisa's viewing pleasure long after Gillian stopped bringing Lisa home.

Besides, the clink of a bat hitting a ball, followed by cheers, was starting to be a feel-good sound—a sound that signaled home, safety, community. Plus, Gillian was quickly becoming a friend. The type of friend who might one day be the *Let's go shopping; how about a movie* type of friend. Lisa had already turned down two invitations to Gillian's church; attending a church softball team sounded safe.

"Yeah, great idea," she agreed. "Let me run upstairs and drop off some stuff."

Gillian followed her up the stairs and into the tiny apartment. She stood in the doorway and looked right, then left. "Wow, I've never seen a place so small."

Lisa tossed her purse onto the tiny kitchen table and headed for the bathroom. "It's perfect for now. I only signed a ten-month lease. Then I'll either know this is the job and place for me and get something bigger or I'll go back to Tucson."

"Don't let Principal Mott hear you say that," Gillian called. "She expects life sentences from her teachers. Look how long Mrs. Henry's been there."

"Longer than I've been alive, and she'll remind you of that every chance she gets." Lisa laughed.

When Lisa left the bathroom, Gillian continued, "Karen, who you're replacing, taught for fifteen years."

"Hmm," Lisa said. "So, besides me, that makes you the new kid on the block."

"Not so new. I attended Sherman Elementary School, my mom was the school nurse—back when the school nurse was a full-time position—and my dad was on the school board. I basically was slated for a position the day I graduated college."

Lisa grabbed a soda, offered one to Gillian, and opened the door to the sound of a ball connecting with a bat. A cheer followed. Gillian grabbed the soda and quickly headed down the stairs.

"Are you in a hurry?" Lisa asked.

Gillian slowed and nodded. "Perry was supposed to get back today. He hasn't called, but he plays on the team. I just want to see if he's back."

Lisa had heard all about Perry Jenson. He worked for the mayor's office and spent more time in Lincoln, Nebraska's capital, than in Sherman.

"What position does he play?" Lisa asked.

"Second base."

That certainly explained why second base had been weak

during practice. The real player had been absent. Lisa hoped there was a good explanation for third base, too. "Why do you suppose he hasn't called?" Lisa asked.

"Oh," Gillian said breezily. "He gets busy."

The team was still warming up when Lisa and Gillian climbed onto the bleachers. Gillian seemed to know everybody and everybody came by to say hi except Perry, who was back in town and busy warming up. There came a round of introductions, complemented by a smattering of *Oh, you're the new first-grade teacher* and ending with a few *You'll be seeing my son, daughter, grandchild, come Monday*.

Before Lisa had time to put faces to names, a man carrying a roster sat down next to Gillian. "We need two more players."

"Not me." Gillian held up a sandaled foot.

He looked at Lisa, and she shook her head. "I'd love to, but I don't belong to your church."

"Belonging to the church is a perk, not a requirement."

"Reverend Pynchon never misses an opportunity," Gillian joked. "Really, thanks for asking, but the last time I played outfield, the ball hit me in the head."

The minister looked at Lisa.

"I play second base."

Wrong thing to say, his eyes lit up.

"I don't have any gear."

"We can provide the gear."

Lisa grinned. "Just tell me when and where."

"Perfect," he said. "We have our team, but I need a few more live bodies, and the list has to go in today. Gillian, can I put your name down, too?"

"Do it, Gillian!" Perry yelled.

Gillian looked trapped.

Lisa took the clipboard from Gillian's hands and dutifully

wrote down her name and number. Slowly, Gillian did the same, but stipulated, "Only call me as a last resort."

He nodded, somebody hollered *Batter up*, and the game began.

A few minutes later, Lisa knew why the preacher's eyes had lit up. Hopefully, Perry was better at politics than he was at softball. The church team was playing the field, and the other team scored three runs with their first three at bats. Perry missed a grounder aimed dead-on at him, one she would have snagged, and also failed to back up the first baseman on another grounder.

Perry didn't act as if he cared that Gillian was in the bleachers. Lisa was about to make a remark about that when she finally noticed the man playing third base.

Greg Bond.

Why had he missed so many practices? Just how dizzy had be been last week? Well, he certainly wasn't dizzy tonight, and he was a pretty good player. Definitely a better player than Perry, and more observant, both when it came to the game and when it came to women. When Lisa—along with a hot dog, a bag of chips and a brownie—settled down to enjoy the game, Greg looked her way. For an unguarded moment, a half grin came to his face. Then, the mask returned and he gave his full attention to third base. For the next half hour, as Lisa finished her hot dog, brownie and purchased another soda, he kept looking her way. It was almost embarrassing.

"See." Gillian nudged her. "He likes you. He's perfect for you, I'm telling you."

"Hush," Lisa said. "He's still wearing his wedding ring. That says it all."

"Perry barely noticed that I'm here," Gillian complained. "One quick wave."

At that moment, two little girls ran toward the fence in front of the bleachers. They hit it hard. A boy was moments behind them. "Daddy!" Amber cried. "I'm hungry."

"Me, too!" the other two cried.

Lisa turned around. Behind her was the playground.

Greg hadn't been checking her out; he'd been keeping an eye on his daughter.

Greg's mind was definitely not on softball. If it had been anything but a church league, he'd have been benched.

His mind was on the bullet, Rachel and Burt.

He'd left work again, claiming dizziness, and had headed home. This time, his boss told him to see a doctor. This time, he didn't have an accident or need to retrieve Amber. He'd scanned the Internet until his eyes were crossed. He'd watched the news until he could recite the same old reports. And after eight hours, all he knew was he needed—no, *deserved*—to bury Rachel properly, and he knew he was slowly losing his mind waiting for Burt to call. Burt had better have something more than what the news channels were reporting.

After making sure the batter wasn't ready, Greg checked his cell phone one more time, just to make sure it was on.

It was—no missed calls.

It was Amber's need to be with other kids and Greg's need to take his mind off his cell phone that drove him out of the house.

It was the wise and healthy choice. It was getting to the point where he wanted to smash his fist right through the screen as he listened to newsman after newswoman read the teleprompter, condemning him.

Unfortunately, softball wasn't enough of a contact sport to take the edge off his anger.

When Lisa showed up at the softball game, Greg noticed but didn't have time to really think about it. He focused on his daughter's whereabouts while listening for the cell phone stashed in his back pocket. He didn't care about the dirty looks his teammates would give him should it ring. He needed to hear what Burt had to say. He wanted to hear that there was some hope of getting his life back!

The first game of the season already hinted at a shutout. The score was 10–2. His team had heart; the other team had a cut-throat mentality.

In some ways, it was Greg's fault. He'd missed every practice. He blamed himself. Somewhere, somehow, he'd really antagonized somebody, and that someone had taken over his life.

Sometimes he didn't feel as if he deserved to have fun. God, it seemed, and the people of Sherman, Nebraska, had other ideas.

The center fielder was the town sheriff, a man named Jake Ramsey who made Greg nervous by his offers of friendship. Even he managed to make it to more practices than Greg, which only implied that it was better to chase criminals than be considered one.

"Batter up!"

Greg glanced over at Amber, then picked up his bat and ambled to the plate. He was able to concentrate by reverting to an old trick. The ball zoomed toward him; it was the bank robber's, the murderer's, head. He swung; the ball clanked at impact, and in a flash Greg went around first, second, third and thundered across home well before the ball made it back to the infield.

He hadn't even realized that two people were on base.

Maybe the game wouldn't be a total embarrassment after all.

"Good going," Perry said. The mayor's assistant had struck out. Looking at the bleachers, Perry did the politician's wave, almost as if he had just homered and driven in three runs.

The sheriff patted Greg on the back. "Way to get us in the game." The applause died down, and Greg looked over to where

Amber was playing. She hadn't noticed the hit, but it looked as if Miss Jacoby and Miss Magee had. They were both smiling as if he'd struck gold.

Miss Magee waved.

Greg looked over at Perry.

The man was an idiot.

If Rachel were here, if Rachel could be cheering Greg on, he would notice. He would hop the fence and give his wife a huge kiss, wave at the fans and grin in satisfaction. Not because of the hit but because of the kiss.

Stop being an idiot, Perry, he urged silently.

The next player made the third out, and Greg trotted to third base. For the next ten minutes he had plenty of time to think because, for some reason, the other team wasn't hitting.

This was his second turn at coed softball with the church's team, thanks to a stubborn minister. And—surprise, surprise— he enjoyed it. Tonight was different. In some ways, he needed to be here, away from the Internet, away from the gut-wrenching fear that tied him to the house and to his memories.

Yup, this was God's way of making sure Greg knew that life was for the living.

When the minister had first approached him about playing on the team, right after Greg had joined the church, Greg said, "No, thanks. I really don't have the time."

Then Amber started in. "Daddy, Tiffany's daddy plays. It's every Friday night and while her daddy plays, her mommy lets Tiffany go to the playground."

Tiffany's mom said the same thing the next Sunday. Then Amber mentioned that her sworn enemy's mother played. "Mrs. Maxwell does first base, Daddy. Mike says she's the best player. I don't really care about that, but I told him you'd be the best." Amber's eyes lit up at this point. "While his mommy's on the field, his daddy watches him on the play-ground. He could watch me, too."

Then Mike's dad made a point of shaking Greg's hand every Sunday. Now *there* was a man with a perfect life. He was a dentist. His wife spent her time taking care of the family, organizing every wedding and baby shower the church put on and playing softball.

The second time the minister approached him, Greg could almost hear Rachel say, "Playgrounds—complete with friends—are a wonderful thing for an only child." Rachel had emphasized over and over that just in case Amy…

Think of her as Amber.

…just in case Amber turned out to be an only child, they had to make sure she did lots of things with friends, kids her age. Outdoor things. Not so much television.

So Greg had joined the team, and even though he hadn't played since high school, he discovered that the team really needed him.

And Amber really needed him playing on the team. Greg looked over at her again. She was having a blast. She'd had a red Sno-Kone and it was all over her face; Mikey looked like someone had dumped a barrel of cherry juice on him. Tiffany managed to look like a princess.

The inning ended. Greg had a while before his turn at bat. He took his cell phone and a hand towel from his bag and, with Amber in tow, headed to a nearby drinking fountain to wash her face.

"I'm not dirty, Daddy."

"No," he agreed. "You're not dirty, you're sticky."

She giggled.

"Why is it," Greg asked, "that Tiffany can eat a Sno-Kone and not get it all over her?"

"Her Sno-Kone is special. Maybe if you buy me another one, this time mine will be special."

He should say no but her eyes were glowing, her cheeks were flushed, and she wasn't suffering.

As he was.

Somehow, in the midst of everything, that brought him to his knees—his daughter was thriving. He handed her a dollar and remembered again why he couldn't turn himself in: two reasons.

One, Greg didn't know if he could face the day without Amber. He'd been a good father while Rachel was alive, but he'd put work first. Now Amber came first and he truly knew the challenge and joys of fatherhood. No way was he playing Russian roulette with the foster-care system.

Which took him to reason number two.

No one would watch Amber with the intensity that Greg did. No one. And Greg knew that *just to get at him,* whoever had killed Rachel wouldn't hesitate to come after Amber.

FIVE

"The media jumped the gun, excuse the pun, by claiming that Rachel and the security guard were 'probably' killed by the same gun," Burt said over the phone late Friday night. "And I'm guessing you missed the word *probably* when you heard the story."

"Most people fail to take note of the word *probably*," Greg responded. "Also, most people figure if the news reported it, it's fact."

"Until the authorities get their hands on the gun, nothing can be proven. What the authorities *do* believe is that both Rachel and the security guard were killed by a 9 mm semiautomatic pistol."

"I didn't own a 9 mm semiautomatic pistol," Greg said.

"What the cops know is that you *didn't* own a *registered* gun. They're not convinced that you didn't get one off the black market."

"Motivation?"

"Getting rid of your family."

"I'm raising my daughter alone! I—"

"Hey, you're preaching to the choir."

"What else do you have?"

"You'll be impressed by what I have, and you should be humbled by what I've given. I owe more favors than I can ever begin to repay. Turn your fax on."

Fifteen minutes later, Burt continued. "Remember, this coroner's report is incomplete. You know I'm a lot more comfortable with skip traces and surveillance than with all this medical stuff. It shouldn't take fifteen pages to report the cause of death."

Greg gripped the fax pages. The coroner's report. It was fifteen pages long only because it was incomplete, and he didn't intend to ask how Burt had got hold of it.

There was Rachel's name, after the word *decedent*. The date of her death was roughly six months ago. Greg noted the names of both the doctor who pronounced her dead and the homicide detective who was assigned to the case.

"So," Greg balanced the phone on his shoulder as he turned a page, "they don't know where she died?"

"They don't—not according to my source and not according to the coroner's report—but they've ruled out your house and they've ruled out the farmhouse."

Greg choked up. "They identified her from dental records. What? She wasn't recognizable?"

"Dental records work well when you're trying to convince a jury. That's all I'm going to say. Don't torture yourself. You remember Rachel the way she was when she and Amy stood side by side.

"Don't let yourself fall apart now," Burt warned. "We're finally moving again, and if we're going to find a light at the end of the tunnel, you're going to have to point to it. Not me, not the police. Remember, I'm not the brainy one. That's you. And, remember, the police are not on your side. They think you robbed your own bank, killed an innocent bystander, killed your wife, kidnapped your own—"

"I get it," Greg snapped.

"Good, because I want you to be angry when you go over every word," Burt said, "so angry that you don't miss a word.

I always liked your wife, and reading this report made me angry all over again."

Burt didn't begin to comprehend the depths of his anguish, Greg thought. The coroner's report shook in his hand. It took a moment, but finally he was able to hold the paper still enough to read. He was listed as next of kin. Their address was listed as the primary residence. The words started to jumble, merge, jump out at him. Words like *marital status, birthplace, trajectory, external examination.* These words were about his wife.

His wife!

When they found her, she was mummified. Her clothes were intact. Her purse, sans wallet, was nearby. She died from a single gunshot wound to the head, through and through. Entry right temple; exit left temple.

Through and through? Words that hadn't made sense at first glance, but made sense when he read more.

Due to Rachel's condition, weight or height were estimated. The coroner thought Rachel had been fairly healthy.

She was! Very healthy. Too healthy to die!

His hands started to shake again, so did the report. On the phone—the forgotten phone—Burt said, "Man, you there? What are you doing? What are you thinking?"

"I'm thinking that I can't do this," Greg whispered softly.

"You already *are* doing it," Burt said. "And because you're doing it, we can catch this idiot and make sure he doesn't destroy anyone else's life."

Greg and Burt had talked through this before. The *hows,* the *whats,* the *whys* and mostly the *whos*. Always they came to the same conclusion. Until they answered those questions, Amber wasn't safe.

"I'm reading about rigor, and the lack of tattoos. I'm reading

about hair color and no joint deformity. I'm reading about…"
He stopped, words jumping out at him, not making sense.

"What? What are you reading about?" Burt practically screamed.

"I'm reading about what they found under her nails."

"Nothing unusual," Burt said. "It's one of the reasons the authorities are so sure the murderer is you—no sign of a struggle."

"Burt, it says here they found makeup under her nails."

"So? Most women have makeup under their nails."

For the first time since they'd found Rachel, Greg felt a smidgeon of hope. "Burt, the only time Rachel wore makeup was when she was in a production. She claimed it did a number on her skin. And she hadn't been in a play since Amy was born."

"You sure?"

"The makeup belonged to the killer. The one disguised to look like me."

On Monday morning, Lisa woke up well before her alarm clock sounded. She tried to go back to sleep, but it wasn't happening. There was way too much to do today!

Lisa's last, somewhat frightening, thought as she ran out of her apartment at the sound of Gillian's horn was, Maybe this is how Mrs. Henry started out.

By eight o'clock, she stood in the middle of twenty-two desks. This was *her* classroom. Okay, so was she going to start every morning with sweaty hands, a forced smile and a dry throat? Oh, come on. She was twenty-three years old and had wanted to be a teacher ever since third grade. Her classroom would make Martha Stewart gush!

Colorful bulletin boards—already marked with birthdays, and just waiting for mention of lost teeth—graced the walls. A reading table and reading centers were in the appropriate corners. The desks were in rows and labeled with the students' names. In a few minutes, twenty-two children would burst through the door, most followed by parents, and she'd start her first day of really, truly being a teacher.

Amber Bond's desk was front row, by the wall. Gillian had forewarned Lisa that Amber definitely liked to look out the window and would rather draw than do anything else.

Gillian, as if knowing that Lisa was thinking about her, poked her head in the doorway. "Hey, ready for your first day?"

"No," Lisa joked. "Do you think they'll give me another day?"

"It depends on who *they* is. School board—no. Principal— no. Students—yes. Parents—no."

"Oh, go away," Lisa scolded.

"Good idea," Gillian said. "I think I'll go make sure everything written on my chalkboard is spelled correctly."

"Kindergartners can't read."

"But their parents can." Gillian laughed all the way down the hallway.

Lisa glanced at her own board.

Clean.

She still had ten minutes. It would fill the time. She picked up the piece of chalk, hoping it would do what standing in the middle of her beautiful room had not: take her mind off her sweaty palms, nervous stomach and dry throat.

"Ahem."

Funny, her handwriting had been perfect until the "Ahem," and, normally, "Ahems" didn't bother her.

Just his did.

"Miss Jacoby, if I could just have a minute."

Greg Bond stood in the doorway to her classroom. He wasn't a big man, but he had presence. His gray-and-white striped shirt, with the name *Greg* embroidered on the left breast, was wrinkled, yet clean, and tucked into dark-blue pants. There was a tear in the knee and what must be a stubborn stain on the bottom of one pant leg.

He needed a woman's touch, definitely. Maybe that would help with the other things, too.

Yikes, where were these thoughts coming from? A woman's touch couldn't help with everything. Her own family was proof of that. One good thing: Greg didn't look unfriendly or distracted today, but the haunted look wasn't so easy to discard.

He only asked for a minute, but she'd willingly give him an hour. "I suppose it's too early to know anything about my car," she said flippantly—wanting to wipe the chalk dust off her fingers but knowing it would just leave streaks on her skirt.

He looked somewhat flustered. Well, good. He flustered her, too, or that *hour* thought wouldn't have surfaced.

"I'm not here about your car—not this time." Absently, he straightened his cap. It advertised Konrad Construction in the same shade of gray as his shirt.

"I guess I should have figured that," Lisa said.

He still looked uncomfortable. "What?"

"I should have figured it wasn't about my car because every time you come to see me about my car, Vince's with you."

He smiled, but it didn't reach those eyes. Too bad, because haunted blue eyes were her weakness. Eyes this shade shouldn't be so sad.

"Amber's out on the playground, and I wanted to talk to you while she wasn't around. I know you've been given the students' records but I wanted to make sure you were clear about Amber's."

"Okay," Lisa said slowly. She was clear, but maybe there was something she'd missed.

"I'm a bit of an overprotective dad. Besides me, the babysitter, Mrs. Griffin, is the only one allowed to pick up Amber. Amber doesn't go to after-school care and she doesn't go home with other children."

"I see," Lisa said slowly. Her first thought was *Yup, he's a hover parent.*

Her second thought was all female: *I wish he'd hover over me.*

Amber was a lucky little girl. "I'll make sure she only leaves with you or Mrs. Griffin," Lisa promised.

His eyes softened, and for the first time Lisa saw what could have been if he weren't so sad.

The morning bell rang. Quick as a wink, the shadows returned to Greg's eyes, and the moment was lost. He backed out of the classroom as students filed in. Most were accompanied by parents. Desks were opened, filled. Tissue boxes gathered on Lisa's desk. Lunch boxes were stacked, backpacks stored, and finally the parents left, leaving Lisa feeling as if she'd just been struck by a small, but fierce, hurricane. The students sat at their desks—except for Mike Maxwell, who was pretty much under his desk.

That first day would forever be a blur. She'd never forget the awe she felt that these were her students and that not one of them wet their pants, not one of them got hurt, not one of them cried and asked to go home or accused her of not being the "real" teacher. They were characters—each and every one—and just like adults, they already had cliques and opinions and habits.

One thing for sure: Amber Bond would never leave the front row. Her self-appointed job was to always know what Mike Maxwell and Tiffany Taylor were doing. Then there was Amber's constant need to draw. It was only when Lisa threatened to put her into time-out that Amber settled down to do reading.

The early morning conversation with Greg Bond stayed with Lisa. By Amber's actions, it was easy to see the effects Greg's hovering had instilled. During recess, Amber never strayed too far from the teacher on duty. During lunch, Amber sat far away from the windows and closest to the lunch monitor. When lining up, Amber—since she didn't pull line-leader duty—made sure she was second in line. Wow. After getting a plate from the lunch lady, Lisa settled down beside Gillian at the teachers' table and whispered, "You said Greg Bond was a protective parent, but it's making Amber a bit needy, don't you think?"

Gillian rubbed her forehead. "Amber is definitely aware of her surroundings, but there are worse things."

"I agree." Lisa took a bite of her hamburger. During her student teaching days and in the classroom, she'd studied children's behavior because of absentee parents. It seemed as if most of the teachers dealt with divorce, parents in jail and students being raised by their grandparents. Lisa couldn't remember spending much time on students grappling with the death of a parent. Still, there were enough similarities.

"I had a little boy show up this morning who wasn't pre-enrolled, who didn't come with a single supply and who doesn't speak a word of English," Gillian said. "He cried all morning, and twice I've had to stop him from running out the door."

A love of drawing, a need to be close to the teacher and keeping track of friends suddenly didn't seem like much of a problem at all.

"What are you doing about it?"

"Mrs. Mott has been in my classroom almost all morning, talking to him and telling him what's going on in class."

Lisa made a mental note: do not ask the principal for help. No way did Lisa want the principal in her class during the first few days when she was feeling her way and would probably stumble a few times. "Mrs. Mott speaks Spanish?"

"Fluently. I wish I knew what she was saying to José. Makes

me long for the time we still had half-day kindergarten. It's what he needs."

By three o'clock, Lisa was ready to head home, sink into a soft chair and call her mother. She'd loved her first day. She didn't mind that she had dried glue on her fingers from helping during art. She didn't mind that her turn at recess duty resulted in a run in her stockings. She didn't mind the chalk streaks on her skirt. And, most of all, she didn't mind hearing "Yes, Miss Jacoby," "Thank you, Miss Jacoby," "You're pretty (or nice, or old) Miss Jacoby," from her students.

Amber was the first to say "Goodbye, Miss Jacoby" as Lisa opened the door to walk the children outside and to the front of the building. She already knew where her assigned space was. Sixth graders, wearing orange vests and calling themselves safety patrol officers, were busy walking little ones to waiting parents. Seasoned parents seemed to prefer waiting in their cars. Other parents, mainly kindergarten parents, stood by the front door. Greg obviously didn't need the help of an eager upperclassman. He was waiting in Lisa's square. Amber looked right and left, and then ran for her dad. He caught her in a bear hug and swung her around. He waited patiently while the three o'clock rush ebbed and until Lisa was down to two students, one of whom suddenly remembered that she was supposed to go to after-school care. Mrs. Mott walked her in. Before Greg could say anything, Amber announced, "Billy's mom is always late picking him up."

"Not," Billy said.

All Greg had to say was "Amber!" and the debate ended.

"What time will you finish here?" Greg asked. "I've been to Vince's brother's garage and your car looks ready. I'm waiting until you take a look at it to write the check."

"I need a half hour to put things away and get ready for tomorrow."

Amber stood. "We'll help! I helped Miss Magee all the time last year."

Which wasn't quite true. Gillian had mentioned that Amber loved to volunteer to help, always got off to a great start, but invariably got sidetracked into either staring out the window or drawing on the newly cleaned chalkboard. Looking at Greg, Lisa expected to see a look of pride, a sparkle in those haunted blue eyes, or something. The only emotion she could see was sadness.

If she thought he'd open up, she'd ask him what caused the sorrow in those blue eyes. She knew, just knew, that if she moved any closer, he'd back away so fast she wouldn't even see him move.

"I'd appreciate the help," Lisa told Amber. "Why don't you go see if anyone left papers or crayons on the floor and then erase the chalkboard."

"We can do that." Greg nodded at Amber.

The door had barely closed on the two before Gillian edged over to Lisa's square and teased, "You sounded a lot like a drill sergeant."

"Oh, no," Lisa protested. "I just had a mentor who—"

But Gillian wasn't done and she obviously didn't want an answer. "Or maybe I should say you sounded a lot like a girl-friend or wife."

"I was talking to Amber, not Mr. Bond," Lisa protested. Luckily, her final charge's parent arrived, and she could head inside before Gillian tried for more.

Under her daddy's supervision, Amber didn't seem to have the "staring out the window" or "drawing on the clean chalk-board" inclination. Greg had the desks in order; Amber had the floor clean; both were currently busy erasing the board. Lisa grabbed some papers off her desk, stuffed them into her bag, and said, "Where to?"

"Vince's brother's place is close to downtown. It will only take us about fifteen minutes to get there."

Greg drove slowly, constantly checking the side streets and his rearview mirror. His technique turned what should have been a ten-minute drive into twenty. Once they pulled into the garage's lot, Vince's brother brought the car to the front, let them look at it, and Lisa had to agree that it seemed good as new. It looked perfect, in fact, as if she'd just driven it off the lot.

Greg wrote a check, apologized one more time and then hustled Amber into his truck. Lisa, holding her car keys in one hand and the receipt in the other, watched them drive away. Greg, once again, was clutching the steering wheel in a death grip. Shrugging, she slid behind the wheel of her vehicle, rolled down the window and enjoyed the idea of not relying on Gillian. First thing, she was off to the grocery store. Then, it was home to a comfortable chair and—

Except her car didn't start. Oh, it turned over, and over and over but it never caught.

Vince's brother came out, held the door open, and Lisa climbed out. After watching him try to start the car, she bent down and said, "So?"

"Something probably came loose. Just sit in the waiting room. I'll get it going."

The waiting room looked like a scene from an old, grainy, black-and-white television show: Black leather couch, complete with jagged tears. Newspapers on the floor. Car magazines on the rickety, brown end tables. She sat facing an old TV, catching the beginnings of the five o'clock news.

The top stories were as gloomy as the waiting room. The news started with a car accident, continued on to the alarming number of foreclosures and finally coasted into the discovery, last week, of a woman's body in an abandoned farmhouse in Yudan, Kansas.

It was footage from the grub bandit robbery Amber had gotten so excited over.

"Ewww," Lisa whispered. She'd been concentrating on Amber and Greg and had only managed a brief look at the grub mask the robber wore. Now she got a good look. About the time her scalp started itching, the news switched photos. Now it showed a picture of Rachel Cooke, the wife of Alex Cooke. She was the elegant, blond, cheerleader type, with enough curl in her hair to make Lisa reach up to stroke her own straight locks.

Then the news segued to a photo of Alexander Cooke, wanted for bank robbery and for killing his wife.

Criminals were supposed to be scary-looking. Not Alexander Cooke. He looked like her sister Tamara's boyfriend, like an urban professional who oozed class and had an agenda of success.

"Hey, your car is ready!" Vince's brother stepped into the room. Before standing to take her keys, Lisa studied the television screen one more time: brown hair, expensive cut; suit, most likely tailor-made; fairly young to be an assistant bank manager. Yup, definitely her sister Tamara's type. Still, for all the glitz, she felt the urge to look even closer.

Alexander Cooke had the most amazing eyes. Dark brown, wide open, smiling at the world and intelligent. Banker eyes— eyes that inspired trust.

Three things kept Greg sane during the month after they discovered Rachel's body. The first was church. Somehow, when he was sitting in the pew, listening to the sermon and trying to keep Amber from whispering, he felt safe. He also felt as if he were taking more from God than he was giving back, but the more he listened to the Word, the more he figured God understood.

Every other day Burt delivered just what Greg needed: a

calming voice and unbiased direction. Burt ordered him to stay in Sherman, pretend nothing happened, act normal. Burt claimed that since the CSI team determined that the makeup found under Rachel's nail was the Ben Nye brand—commonly used by makeup artists and actors—for the first time the authorities had to address doubt that Alexander Cooke was the killer.

They, of course, tried to address this new fact by accusing Greg of wearing makeup.

Only thing was that none of the bank employees thought he was wearing any, and even the arresting officer, the same one who'd lost track of Greg during the interrogation, didn't recall Greg looking like he wore makeup.

Hope—Greg felt hope as he listened to the preacher teaching from the first book of Samuel about David being so afraid. Well, if David could be afraid, so could Greg. David was afraid of the King of Gath. Greg was afraid of an unknown killer and of known authorities.

David had loyal followers who knew he was good. Greg had Amber and Burt. David, in order to avoid death at Gath's hands, pretended to be insane. Greg, in order to avoid arrest, was also pretending to be something, someone, he wasn't.

It was enough to drive him insane.

Thanks to the church, he didn't have to feel alone as he battled this invisible foe.

Loneliness had been an issue from the time he was ten and his mother hadn't come home. He'd knocked on a neighbor's door after two weeks of getting himself to school, getting himself meals and getting himself to bed. He *could* take care of himself, but once the electricity was shut off and the food disappeared, it all became too much.

His neighbor, an elderly woman who'd meant well, had called the police. They'd done a cursory search for his mother and then he'd been assigned to a group home. The group home segued into more foster care homes than he could count: some good—why didn't they last? Some bad—why couldn't he erase them from his memory? The only positive thing that came from the foster-care system, besides a brief introduction to God, was Burt Kelley, another foster kid who managed to travel the same route as Greg. They'd shared three assignments: two bad, one good. They'd lost touch at eighteen when first Burt, then Greg, aged out of the foster-care system.

Burt had entered a life of crime; Greg had entered college.

Both had the weight of the world on their shoulders and no one to turn to. During Greg's junior year of college, he'd met Rachel and said goodbye to loneliness. Then, when Amy was born, he'd almost put the memory of what it felt like to be truly alone behind him.

Almost.

He knew now what he hadn't then. That to truly shed the feeling of loneliness, he needed to know that God was with him, had always been with him, even through the darkest days.

Funny, it had been during a sermon about tithing that, in boredom, he'd stumbled across the verses that became his creed. Isaiah, chapter 41, to be exact: *Fear thou not; for I am with thee; be not dismayed; for I am thy God: I will strengthen thee; yea, I will help thee; yea, I will uphold thee with the right hand of My righteousness.*

Greg had never really believed in epiphany, but he recognized a helping hand when one was offered. It was at that moment that he truly knew God existed, and that he would make it. Then God did something no one else could have done. He offered more, in the form of a Bible verse: *Behold, all they that were incensed against thee shall be ashamed and confounded; they shall be as nothing; and they that strive with thee shall perish.* And, Greg Bond knew that he'd just been handed the strength to go on.

Almost from the moment Greg had entered the Main Street Church—on Burt's orders to be noticed—Greg had been petitioning God in prayer, but never before had he so recognized God's answering.

Church was Greg's sanctuary, his respite, his tiny slice of peace on earth.

He looked forward to Sundays and Wednesdays. He halfway looked forward to Friday, although he didn't quite feel safe on the softball field. But sometimes, right after he checked Amber's whereabouts and made a good play, he felt a sense of contentment, that everyday life was trying to reestablish itself.

It wasn't going to happen.

Not while the killer was still on the loose.

Softball also put him in contact with Amber's first-grade teacher. Someone Greg saw—and thought of—way too often. She came to every game and sat next to Gillian Magee.

Gillian, of course, came to cheer on Perry. She was the ultimate fan. Miss Jacoby came to keep Gillian company. At least, that's what he told himself. He wasn't blind, deaf or dumb. He knew an attraction—on both sides—simmered just beneath the surface. But, oh my, was she an innocent. She tended to blush the moment she saw him. And, for his part, he avoided her.

Yet, his daughter loved school, and if ever there were a time Greg needed Amber to feel safe, it was now. Seeing her daddy's picture on the news put Amber back to clinging just when she'd somewhat stopped. She was also back to calling for him in the middle of the night. Even worse, she was back to calling for her mother.

That Friday, when they arrived home, Amber hurried inside

to put her things away and get out her Barbies. Greg headed straight to the computer to see if there were any updates on Rachel's case. He also kept checking voice mail to see if he might have missed a call from Burt. Burt had camped out in Yudan, Kansas, where Rachel's body had turned up, for all the good it did. The person pretending to be Alex hadn't left a pencil this time. No, instead, he'd left makeup smears under Rachel's fingernails. He'd also left a few hairs that weren't his. That info hadn't made the news. Burt, as only someone with connections could, lucked into it. Greg's hair was found at the scene.

Did that mean that when the man broke into Greg's house *to kill his wife,* he'd taken the time to either steal a comb or just swipe a few strands from the comb? Because the hairs were found near the flowers and not on the body, the authorities didn't believe the hairs had traveled to the burial site with Rachel's body.

A good defense lawyer would claim that "Of course, Greg's hairs were on Rachel. He was her husband. He hugged her, slept with her, etc."

Maybe without the hair as evidence, the makeup traces would have made more of a difference. Maybe then he'd not still be enemy number one.

The bank robbery, combined with two murder charges, would have netted Alex life or the death penalty. Either way, once everything was said and done, he'd be in his mid-thirties by the time he was sentenced. He'd be around to hear about Amber's first date; he'd see her high school graduation announcement and know the name of the man she married.

He'd live to see what his wife didn't: his daughter grow up.

"Daddy, will you read this to me?" Amber's voice brought him back to the present. Man, how long had he been staring at the computer screen?

He should have been playing with his daughter instead. None of this was her fault, and yet she was paying the price, too. No mother and a distracted father.

He watched as she dug into her backpack and found the end-of-the-week update from Miss Jacoby. Amber handed him the *First Grade News* and the simple gesture reminded him that she, *not some insane impersonator,* was all that mattered in life.

"Of course, I'll read it," Greg said. "I can hardly wait." He meant it, too. Last year, in kindergarten, Mrs. Magee simply typed out her Friday updates and requests. Miss Jacoby was more creative. No wonder his daughter was as enraptured as he was. *The First Grade News* looked like a newsletter. Across the top were dancing children. Amber always colored them. Miss Jacoby spelled out what the students were working on. Next week, the class would celebrate the letter D.

As in *death penalty.*

It also looked like Sherman Elementary was wasting no time before scheduling Open House Night. It was Thursday.

Oh, and show-and-tell started this coming Tuesday.

Greg dutifully read each word to Amber. Her eyes lit up on show-and-tell. "Can I take a picture of Mommy?"

She knew better. He'd explained over and over. It was on the tip of Greg's tongue to say, "Honey, you know better." But the more he parented alone, the more he knew not to trust the tip of his tongue. So instead he made a promise to himself. He'd be more involved, more easygoing, for Amber's sake. Instead, he said, "You can't take Mommy's picture yet. Right now we don't know what's going to happen because of the bank robbery. We just might get to hang her pictures on every wall and even go home if they find the bank robber, but until they do we have to be even more careful."

Amber nodded. Her blue eyes—no way was he making her wear contacts she didn't need—started to fill with tears.

"Oh, baby, I promise, someday we'll put Mommy's picture right where it needs to be."

"That's not it, Daddy."

"Then what is?"

"You said we might get to go home when they catch the bank robber." Now the tears were really falling. "I don't know where *home* is."

As Greg gathered her in his arms and rocked her, he suddenly realized that he no longer knew, either.

SIX

"Perry won't be back in time to play tonight," Gillian said as she walked into Lisa's classroom. The two were quickly becoming a team. Half the time, Lisa headed for Gillian's classroom to share an anecdote or activity. Gillian reciprocating the other half of the time. Fridays were always the longest day as teachers had to clean up from the week just past and prepare for the upcoming one.

The first month of school had been one adventure after another. Every day Lisa fell more in love with her profession, but every day she missed her sisters and her mother more. Which is why she was so glad that tonight would see her out on the field doing something different, being part of a team.

"I know. Your minister called and asked me to play second base. It's been more than a year since I've played." Lisa wasn't worried, though. Softball always felt natural to her. All in all, it was the perfect end of her first full month of teaching. She knew every kid's name, she had the kids somewhat under control, and she was learning which parents went with which kid. Yup, she definitely felt like a "real" teacher. And now getting to play second base was icing on the cake. She could almost feel the excitement.

"I'll be there to cheer you on."

"Did the minister ask you to play?"

"Yes, but I told him the only thing I want to do with a soft ball—notice I'm making that two words instead of one—is aim it at a cat."

"So, what's so important that Perry can't make it back?"

Since the first Friday night, back in late August, and through September, Lisa and Gillian had been regular fans at the softball game. Gillian cheered for Perry, both when he snagged a ball or, more often when he missed. As she did for her kindergartners, she always found something to praise.

Lisa figured the kindergartners were easier to please.

They cheered for Greg, too, because no one ever seemed to be there for him except Amber.

Perry took it in stride, as if it were his due. Greg, well, Greg looked uncomfortable. It was charming, really.

"There's some event at the courthouse, and Perry is expected to attend," Gillian said.

"And he couldn't bring a date?"

"Oh, he could, but there's no way I could finish work and make it up there and get my clothes and hair right. He thinks that, after we're married, I'll quit my job." Gillian bit her lip. "I'm not sure I will, though."

"It's something you'd better discuss now," Lisa advised as she put the last of her papers into her bag. "And why is he talking marriage if he hasn't even given you a ring?"

Gillian was silent for a moment. "We used to talk marriage. We haven't for a while. That's why I've gone back to calling him my boyfriend instead of my fiancé."

Lisa waited to see if Gillian would say anything else, and when she didn't, Lisa finally said, "I need to hurry home and collect my gear. Meet me at the park, and we'll grab a bite there."

Friday night hot dogs during the game were becoming a

tradition. Only tonight Lisa needed to eat before the game and early enough that she didn't feel full while she played.

Two hot dogs later, Lisa put on her glove—it had traveled all the way from Arizona, courtesy of Lisa's mother and the U.S. Postal Service—and headed out to practice. It took a few minutes, but after a few solid throws and a decent catch or two, she was as ready as she would ever be. And easily part of the team. Mikey's mother shook her hand. And the three outfielders, all siblings—two brothers, one sister—asked her what size they should order her T-shirt.

Okay, she could wear a T-shirt with giant letters that read *We Rock Because We Follow the Rock* and which had a cartoonish baseball player standing on a rock as a visual.

Medium, she wore a medium.

The minister, who played catcher, beamed. "I knew you were a find. Tell me you can bat, and I'll know my prayers are answered."

"I can bat."

Greg showed up minutes before the start of the game. He jogged to the outfield without doing even one practice throw and checked for Amber's whereabouts. Lisa followed his gaze and saw Amber chasing Mikey around the slide. When Mr. Maxwell joined in the chase, Greg relaxed.

That's when he noticed her on second.

And did a double take.

She grinned. At first she thought his surprised reaction was due to Perry's absence and her taking his spot. But after a moment she knew it was because of the way she looked. There were some men who like seeing a woman in cutoff jeans and a T-shirt advertising the Arizona Diamondbacks. There were some men who liked ponytails that poked out of the back of baseball caps.

Greg was one of them.

She couldn't see the blue eyes that usually spoke volumes to her, always saying something about sadness and pain, but she could see the hint of a grin and the tilt of his head. It was enough.

"Hey!" she called. "I hope you're ready to finally win a game!"

They were down 0–5. The first night had been the only time they'd even come close with a 3–7 game.

"Oh," Greg teased. "You think you're that good."

"I *know* I'm that good."

Before he could respond, the umpire called "Batter up," and the game began. For Lisa, being in the game felt like Christmas. There was something about the end of September in Nebraska, a crispness in the air or maybe it was the brilliant sunsets. She felt alive. So much so that the homesickness that had been nipping at her heels for the last few weeks dissipated. Energy and happiness took its place.

First inning she caught a pop fly.

Third inning Greg hit a double.

Sixth inning she both caught the ball and tagged a player: a double play, thanks to her. Not to be outdone, Greg snagged a grounder for the third out.

Ninth inning, Greg hit a single with the bases loaded. Lisa—who was on third—made it to home plate and the game was over. Eight to seven, the Rocks won.

Once she hit the dugout, handshakes and slaps on the back abounded, except from Greg. As her enthusiasm grew, so did his. And, boy, did she notice. He didn't offer a handshake or a slap on the back, only a grin. But she knew. She watched him every morning and late afternoon as he cared for his daughter. She'd watched him play ball for the last five weeks, and tonight he'd put his heart in it and she knew, just knew, it was because of her.

They made a good team.

"Everyone for pizza!" the minister yelled. "I'm not taking any no's this time. That goes for you, Greg. And Lisa, since this was your first game, we're treating."

"Sounds good," Lisa said. Pizza after the game was tradition. She'd heard the invitation before, but since Perry always declined with an *I'm tired* excuse, she'd never gotten to tag along.

Greg zipped his bag and offered the same refusal he'd given for the last five weeks. "Not tonight."

"We won!" Lisa argued. "And it's not a school night—"

"Yeah, Daddy, it's not a school night." Amber rushed into the dugout. "Mikey said you won the game! Did you, Daddy?"

He ruffled the top of her hair. "Well, I didn't do it alone, but yes, we won the game by one point, thanks to your teacher."

"Oh, no," Lisa protested. "I may have touched home plate, but Tiffany's mommy hit the ball."

"Tiffany's going for pizza," Amber said mournfully.

Greg shook his head. "Tonight's not—"

"Mike's going for pizza."

"And we'll go some other time, but, Amber—"

"Are you going for pizza?" Amber looked at Lisa.

Probably, she should have let him off the hook. But, hey, she was human, and he was cute. "Of course I'm going. We won!"

Amber looked pointedly at her father.

He sighed. When he looked at Lisa, though, his eyes weren't sad or pained, he looked like a dad who'd just lost a small battle and was almost glad he'd lost.

"Oh," Lisa added, teasingly, "make sure our cars don't meet in the parking lot, okay?" With that, she flounced her hair and hurried over to Gillian.

"My, my," said Gillian, "what was that all about?"

"The team's heading over to One Stop Pizza. I even talked

Greg into going. Come on, we'll take my car and I'll bring you back afterward."

Lisa didn't have to ask twice. Gillian gathered her stuff and in a matter of moments they were in the car, all the while with Gillian muttering, "I keep telling Perry he should join everyone for pizza, but he's too busy."

"Then go without him. You're part of that church. They love you."

"I couldn't go without him. It would just cause an argument later."

Lisa pursed her lips. Truth was, she'd never been in a serious relationship. She'd been too focused on school and fun. She'd watched both her sisters, though. Tamara, the lawyer, would have served him with *"We're-so-over"* papers by now, and Sheila, the author, would have killed him off during chapter two—make that their second date. Shaking her head, she accused, "You guys have been dating seriously for how long?"

"Oh, okay, fine, I'll go eat pizza. But Perry and I have been serious for almost six years and we've known each other forever."

"And half the time you don't tell him how you really feel."

"It will be easier after we're married. Then, he'll *have* to listen."

Lisa glanced down at Gillian's bare ring finger. The amazing Perry had promised a ring *when he got around to it.* Lisa bit back the words that threatened to come out. Men didn't change. For a marriage to work, both parties had to work together, adapt, not so much change.

Lisa's mother, Judy Jacoby, had planned on Richard Jacoby changing after marriage, too. She'd married him a month after high school, had three children right in a row and then spent fifteen years trying to convince her husband that she'd rather be wed to a familyaholic than a workaholic.

Her dad died just before he turned forty.

Big sister, Tamara, looked and acted just like Dad.

Middle sister, Sheila, was a mix.

And Lisa, the baby, was her mother all over again. Everyone said so. She believed firmly in happily ever after. But, thanks to a father she barely remembered, maybe even while she was looking for true love, she didn't quite believe it was possible.

Greg Bond just might be the ticket. He was not a workaholic who put family second. He always dropped off and usually picked up his daughter.

Only he worried too much, and his eyes always seemed filled with such sadness.

She wanted to know why.

"Well," Gillian demanded. "Aren't you going to say anything else?"

Lisa shook her head. She was afraid to, because although she was the sister who believed in happily ever after, she was the one sister who'd never managed to hold on to a relationship for more than a month.

What right did she have to give advice to Gillian?

One Stop Pizza looked full, so Lisa was somewhat astonished at how easily the softball team entered, found a table and fit in. With Jake Ramsey, the town's sheriff, on one side and Gillian on the other, Lisa soon watched in amazement as more than twenty people—including spouses and kids—bowed their heads in a prayer most couldn't even hear. Then, before she knew it, she was eating a piece of pizza she shouldn't be hungry for and also getting two offers of marriage. One came from the sheriff. With a quick glance at Greg, Jake claimed he'd be doing Sherman a favor by eliminating her as a distraction.

"I wasn't distracted," Greg muttered. "I was in a hurry."

The other proposal came from the preacher. Oh, not for

himself: his wife wasn't a backup on the softball team this season because son number five was all of four weeks old. The preacher, it seemed, had a brother. And, the preacher reasoned, if he got Lisa in the family, she'd have to stay on the team.

The sheriff started to propose to Gillian, but she gave him a her very best stern-teacher look. She gave Lisa an equally stern look when Lisa pointed out her *no ring, no commitment* theory.

Greg and Amber were across from Lisa, wedged up against each other, and Greg managed to look amused while Amber giggled. Tiffany and Amber were carefully picking all evidence of sausage from the pizza and, when Dad wasn't looking, tossing them at Mike.

And to think she'd thought religious people were dull. By the time Lisa finished her fourth and final piece of pizza, One Stop was fairly empty. Greg loosened up and let the girls follow Mike's lead and go to the play area. Then he leaned forward and surprised Lisa by instigating a conversation. Oh, not with her, but with the men. The topic: Nebraska getaway spots. Jake's favorite was in Valentine, Nebraska. The preacher preferred a little town called Prairie. Lisa had never heard of it. Seemed Greg hadn't either, judging by all the questions.

Gillian had, but didn't think much of it. "Nothing to do," she grumbled.

"That's the point," the preacher said.

At that moment, Lisa felt pressure against the back of her chair, and she turned around just in time to see who gruffly spoke the words, "Hey, I didn't expect to find you here."

The words, however, weren't meant for her. They were aimed at Gillian. Perry, still in a suit and tie and clutching a newspaper, leaned against Lisa's chair and looked at Gillian.

Her face lit up. Ah, the look of love. Gillian jumped up, took

Perry's hand and looked one way then the other before saying, "Let's find a spot together, just the two of us."

She headed for a dark booth in a back corner, but Perry dug his heels in, literally. "Let's stay here with the team."

Lisa recognized the look on his face. It was similar to the one her sister Tamara used in the courtroom. It was meant to intimidate. Only no one looked intimidated. Gillian, however, looked stricken.

Taking pity, Lisa stood. "You can have my spot, Perry." It wasn't until she rounded the table and took Amber's vacated place that she realized that two little girls didn't equal one big girl, and the change of location put her wedged up against Greg. He looked at her, and she thought he touched her leg. It's what a friend would have done, acknowledging that he recognized just what she'd maneuvered, but Greg didn't look comfortable enough to have touched her leg.

Must have been her imagination.

"So," Perry said, taking the last piece of pizza. "How much did we lose by?"

"We didn't lose," the preacher gushed. "We won by a point."

"I made the hit," Annie Maxwell bragged.

"And Lisa made the winning run," Greg said.

Perry nodded while removing the sausage from his pizza. "Did we play one of the new teams?"

"No," Annie said. "We played the Athletics."

Perry looked like he'd swallowed a lemon. The Athletics were a team from the local gym. They weren't as good as they should be, considering all the muscle and brawn they brought to the field, but every year they usually manage to win a trophy or two. "They must have really relaxed when they heard they were playing us."

"No," Greg said. "We just played a good game."

"We were a team," Annie said.

"We rocked!" the preacher added, emphasizing his T-shirt.

"And that reminds me," Annie said, looking over at where the kids were playing. "It's almost ten, and although I no longer rock Mike to sleep, pretty soon I'm going to have to carry him to the car and he weighs more than a rock."

The preacher collected the money—Lisa noticed that Perry didn't chip in, although Gillian did—and soon sweaters were put back on, purses gathered and goodbyes said.

Amber protested, "But I don't want to go home yet" in the same tone that Tiffany was whining, "But I'm not tired." Mike was in his dad's arms and it looked as if he were shaking his head at the females' finagling.

"It's time to go home," Greg said to Amber. "And if you want to convince me to come again, you'll clean up some of the sausage mess you and Tiffany made."

Amber's eyes went wide. Clearly, she hadn't realized that Daddy was aware of what they had done. She hit the floor, knees smashing more sausage than she picked up, and started cleaning. Greg picked up his hat from the table, and then, for a moment, fingered Perry's newspaper. To Lisa, it looked like Greg's knees buckled.

"Are you all right?" she asked.

"I think I'm as tired as the littlest Maxwell," he joked. The forced smile didn't last. A moment later, Greg herded Amber out the door. Lisa picked up her purse and looked for Gillian. Chances were Perry would give Gillian a ride home, but Lisa wanted to make sure.

They were arguing in the dark booth Gillian had wanted to move to earlier.

Okay, best to stick around for a few minutes. Sitting at the empty table, Lisa gathered the dirty napkins and brushed aside bits of cheese and a mound of sausage bits. Perry's newspaper lay in the middle of the table. Picking it up, she tried to see what Greg had been looking at that made him go so white.

It was Lincoln's main paper. The front page looked like any would. The biggest photo featured a politician, probably one of Perry's cronies. The accompanying story was too boring to read. Gas prices were skyrocketing. Greg drove a truck. Maybe he was worried. There'd been a flood in one of the Eastern states. Did Greg have family? No, surely he'd have said something. Ah, the stock market took a crash. That had to be it. Gillian said Greg was the best dad when it came to figures. He'd tallied her Fall Festival's booth earnings last year to the penny. He'd also been the only dad to turn in the right amount of money during both school fund-raisers. Her sister Tamara dabbled with investments and turned white when she read the stock listings, too.

Lisa didn't have the money or the know-how to play the market. Plus, she hadn't inherited her father's "A penny saved today is a dollar spent tomorrow" philosophy.

It only took one glance in Gillian's and Perry's direction for Lisa to realize that it would be a long night. Perry stood stiffly and as he spoke, he pointed a finger at Gillian. Gillian had her arms folded one over the other and her lips were pursed in anger, even as she glared in turn at Perry's finger and then at his face. Good, she wasn't giving in.

Folding the paper in half, Lisa looked at the final front-page story. It was about the woman whose body had been discovered last month in a deserted farmhouse. The television news had moved on, but sometimes the paper still provided updates. This one looked more like a human-interest follow-up than a news story. It focused on the Internet and how all across America people were still weighing in on whether Alex Cooke was indeed the murderer. The journalist provided a few comments from Internet sites and noted that sites that required "real" names seemed to get thoughtful comments while sites that allowed anonymous posters often got long-winded rants, off-topic issues, or statements that made no sense at all.

The first comment cited merely said, *If Alex Cooke is caught, he should receive the death penalty, and justice should be swift. In other words, our tax dollars should not care for this bank killer for sixteen years while he plays with the system.* Another comment stated, *White collar criminals are always let off. The police know where Alex Cooke is. They've been paid off to keep silent.* The next comment was actually sympathetic to Cooke. *Alex Cooke dose not have a crimnal record. He obviously is mentaly ill. He needs help not jaletime.* Okay, so the poster couldn't spell. Lisa shook her head. The journalist had tallied the number of comments condemning Cooke and the number of comments supporting him. Most seemed to consider the man guilty.

Lisa gasped at the final example. It didn't really fit under any category, except maybe scary. Some insane person had posted the following rhyme to a public forum: *You can run but you can't hide. You're the reason your wife died.*

It took Burt three days to find out what the cops weren't saying and finally call Greg with an update. They'd traced the blog comment to a library in Lawrence, Kansas, his wife's hometown, a mere hour from Wellington and Greg's old bank. The library had multiple computers; they couldn't determine which computer had been used. They did know that their fugitive had opened a new account, made the same comment on thirty different sites, and hadn't commented since. The library did keep a sign-in sheet. Even they weren't impressed with its accuracy.

"Probably someone who doesn't have a nine-to-five job or who doesn't mind calling in sick," Burt said. He actually sounded upbeat. "That fits the profile for a typical bank robber."

"And my name is not on that list?" Greg balanced his phone between his shoulder and ear, and looked at a comment on a news columnist's site.

"Your name is not on the list," Burt answered. "I'm thinking this is one of our best leads yet. I've spoken with the head librarian, Shelly Moser. She knows what you look like. She says you were not in the library that day, or ever for that matter. Says Rachel would come by every time she visited Lawrence, for old times' sake. Apparently Rachel even brought Amber along once or twice, introduced her to everyone."

Greg closed his eyes. He couldn't even say how many times Rachel had gone back to Lawrence for a weekend visit. He'd worked so much before his death.

Burt continued, "Mrs. Moser has a memory like a steel trap. She was telling me things about you and Rachel that even I didn't know."

"My wife grew up in Lawrence, went to school in Lawrence and her parents died in Lawrence. We were married in Lawrence."

"I know," Burt said. "And now this case has a powerful connection to Lawrence, *to Rachel*. I told you more than a month ago that I wanted to go back into Rachel's past. I got sidetracked in Yudan. I'm heading to Lawrence tomorrow. I figure with what we *do* know, maybe I can narrow the field."

"Lawrence is good-sized. It's not Wellington."

"I'm aware of that," Burt said drily. "But I'll limit my questions to near the library and near where Rachel lived, worked and went to school. Our guy is not a typical bank robber. He did not rob your bank for money—he robbed your bank to get at you, I'm guessing because of Rachel. That, actually, gives me some idea of who I'm looking for. We have a computer-savvy man who doesn't work on Friday afternoons and who is most likely from Kansas. He's about your height and build. He knows a lot about you and Rachel—especially Rachel."

To Greg's way of thinking, most people in his age group were computer savvy. Then, too, finding out that the bank robber didn't work nine-to-five seemed like a pretty weak lead. Off the top of his head, he could name ten guys, really good guys, he'd graduated college with who either worked from home or who traveled or who worked evenings. Greg was five-ten, average height, and had always considered himself lean, even with his newly acquired construction worker's bulk. That the bank robber was from Kansas seemed almost predictable. That the bank robber might be from Lawrence was not.

Nothing else about the man indicated typical bank robber, besides possibly being unemployed. He wasn't nonwhite, he wasn't—as far as they could tell—a repeat offender. He didn't act as if he were on drugs.

This bank robber acted alone. Plus, it seemed that the man who had robbed Alex's bank wore not one but two masks—the first a grub mask; the second an Alex Cooke mask.

"I intend to stay on the Lawrence angle," Burt said. "I'm more convinced than ever that the bank robber is someone you or your wife knew. If it's convenient, I plan to leave Lawrence on Saturday morning and head up to Sherman, meet with you, show you some things and maybe delve a little more into the months before your wife's murder. We're missing something."

"Thanks, Burt. I'll see if the sitter can watch Amber on Saturday."

"Good," Burt said. "We have a lot to talk about. And—" as if he knew what Greg were thinking "—stop blaming yourself. It's not your fault that Rachel was killed."

Greg managed to croak a goodbye. Hanging up the phone, he wondered how many times the rhyme would run through his head before he lost his mind. *You can run but you can't hide. You're the reason your wife died.* Greg had found all thirty places. He'd simply done an Internet search for his "real" name and there it was. It made him wonder just what was out there he hadn't stumbled across yet.

"Daddy, are you taking me to school?" Amber walked into his office and plopped down in front of the television. He bit his lip as she hit the "on" button. But she must have been watching the television last night, because cartoons flared to life.

He was afraid to watch the news.

Would there ever be a day when he didn't expect the worst? Didn't worry that his own daughter might someday realize just what her daddy was accused of?

"Did you eat breakfast?" he asked.

She shook her head. The girl ate like a bird, except when it came to snacks.

"Which do you want? Pancakes or cereal?"

"Cereal."

Before leaving his office, he flipped open his datebook. It was the last day of September. A whole new month dawned. He was set for work all month. Plus, he had Sherman Elementary school's Open House this Thursday, and one week later he had a late-afternoon parent/teacher conference.

He made the cereal and then, just to keep Amber company, poured a bowl for himself. He noticed that if he ate with her, she tended to eat a bit more.

"Is there anything special I should know about Open House, besides what Miss Jacoby's newsletter tells me?"

"Zoe Webster has the chicken pox so I get to be in the play."

"What play?"

"The one we're doing during Open House." Her eyes lit up. "It's in the main auditorium. It's about the school day. I get to play a teacher. I have two lines. I get to say, 'Please eat your whole sandwich' and 'Three o'clock, class dismissed.'"

"When did all this happen?"

"Yesterday. Miss Jacoby picked me because I already knew all the lines. She says I'm a natural."

"Then why weren't you in the play in the first place?"

"Each grade only got to have two kids in the play. Miss Jacoby asked who wanted the parts. Everybody, even Mikey, raised their hands. So Miss Jacoby put our names in a jar and drew."

"Sounds fair."

Amber shrugged. "Maybe. She left the rest of the names in the jar. She said she'd use them the next time something special came up and she had to pick."

"Do you need to be there early?"

"Yes." Amber eyed him with disdain, such a little-girl look. "There's a note in my backpack. Didn't you see it?"

"No, probably because you didn't tell me to look for it."

"Daaaaad."

"Don't *dad* me." Greg fetched the backpack and took out folders, pens, wrinkled papers, an apple with one bite missing. Five library books, all overdue. No wonder the pack weighed a ton. "Is it in one of the folders?" he asked.

"No." Amber took one last bite of her cereal and then pulled the backpack toward her. Unzipping a side pocket, she withdrew a note and more.

The note mentioned Amber's part. The copy of the play went a little further. The make-believe teacher even had a name: Miss Smith. The lines Amber needed to say were underlined. All the little actors and actresses were to meet in their homerooms before Open House started.

Greg stared at the paper. How many times had he dropped Rachel off at rehearsals back when they were first married? She'd seemed content with secondary roles and walk-on parts. She'd love to dress up. Looked like Amber was a chip off the old block.

"Miss Jacoby even has a costume for me," Amber gushed. "I get to dress like a teacher!"

Two days later, Greg pulled into the parking lot of Sherman Elementary. Some parents obviously didn't know that those who arrived a half hour early deserved a primo parking spot. Greg found himself parking in the north forty. Amber bounced in the passenger seat. Her face flush with excitement. She'd practiced her lines the whole way over. Not only was Greg now hungry for a sandwich, but he was pretty sure he'd never again need reminding that school ended at three o'clock.

Amber waited impatiently while he locked the car. Then, taking his hand, she hurried him to the front entrance. Clearly, if she didn't make it on time, the show might not go on!

Amber burst into the classroom and gave Miss Jacoby a hug. Gone was the nervous woman who'd created a perfect classroom. In her place stood a woman who had created a haven for her students.

Greg was grateful.

"You're on time," she said.

"Of course."

She chuckled. Tonight she wore a blue-and-white-checked dress and simple white shoes. Her red hair just missed her shoulders, curling under, and bounced slightly as she continued chuckling.

Greg blinked, the attraction hitting him full force and making him take one step backward. No way, no how—talk about bad timing.

Unaware of his angst, Lisa kept talking, her words soft,

soothing, feminine, and a little teasing. "Well, you always seem to show up one minute before the softball game starts, so I was a little worried."

It used to feel natural to smile. Now every time he felt his lips forming the familiar shape, he felt guilty. Still, Amber was too cute not to smile at. And, well, so was her first-grade teacher.

"The softball game is a daddy reward. I manage to get there. Tonight—the play—it's a little-girl reward. You'd better believe I'd get her here on time."

They both looked at Amber. She sat at her desk, taking out drawings. Then Greg glanced back at Miss Jacoby.

She was watching him.

Probably in much the same way he was watching her. Definitely the way a single woman looked at a single man.

He was single.

And it had only taken a single bullet to put him that way.

He'd already taken one step, now he took the rest, right out the door. "I'll go to the auditorium and make sure I get a good seat."

She blushed.

The auditorium was only about a quarter filled. A student handed him a program. He read it as he walked past all the parents—mother and father combos—into the room.

At seven, everyone was to meet in the auditorium. Good, he was early. It gave him a chance to check out everything. No one appeared suspicious.

Greg tried to relax. This night was for Amber. There would be a short program, complete with a talk by the principal. He liked Mrs. Mott. She was no-nonsense and got things done, unlike Miss Jacoby.

Blue-and-white-striped dress. She looked straight out of *Hee Haw*. Yesterday, during the afternoon, Miss Jacoby had the class make the bird feeders. They'd used pinecones as a stabilizer. Last night, Amber spent hours mixing together all the peanut butter and honey in the house. Nothing Greg said could convince her that a million hungry birds were not heading in their direction.

At Greg's house, though, pinecones were at a premium. All he really had on hand that would work were toilet paper rolls.

He now had at least twelve rolls of toilet paper that were roll-less.

He felt her soft touch on his hand even before he noticed her crouched beside him and heard her whisper. "Mr. Bond, we've got a problem."

He tensed, his mind immediately sifting through scenarios from Amber accidentally letting slip her "real" name to her teacher to Amber having vanished. He stood, ready to run for the classroom, grab his daughter and disappear. Before he took a step, Miss Jacoby, looking sheepish asked, "Has Amber complained about not feeling well?"

"No," he blurted. "She's been flushed all evening, but I thought it was from excitement."

He sat, amazed at the panic he'd felt and somewhat dizzy at the realization that he'd almost overreacted. Of course, they didn't have a doctor. He'd been terrified to take her. If she were sick, he'd—

"Mr. Bond, it's all right," Miss Jacoby said. "Well, it's not all right. Amber's not going to be able to perform tonight. She has the chicken pox."

SEVEN

Amber didn't come to school on Friday.

The little girl's absence made Lisa realize that she was becoming too close, too soon. All day, she worried about Amber. Then again, she worried about all five of her students who were out absent. But the only one she wanted to call and check up on was Amber.

Did Greg even know what to do about chicken pox, since he didn't even have a clue that his daughter had come down with it?

Fathers were funny. Her own dad had never been around when she and her sisters were sick. He'd left his wife to deal with it. The most Lisa could remember him doing was coming in, feeling her forehead and saying, "You'll be fine."

Come to think of it, she'd believed him.

Friday night, Greg didn't show up for softball. On the one hand, she hadn't expected him. On the other hand, she didn't know how to deal with the rush of disappointment his absence inspired.

Unfortunately, Perry did show up.

The minister, sitting on the bench and muttering something about *not needing this on their next-to-last game* asked Lisa, "Can you throw from third to first?"

Perry didn't give her a chance to answer. "I can."

Glancing first at Gillian, who was tying her shoes and giving her a beseeching look, Lisa said, "It's been a long time. I'm not sure."

"Okay," the minister said. "Perry, you're on third. Lisa, same as last week, you're on second. Then I'm pulling our right fielder in to play first. Gillian, that puts you in right field."

"Pray for rain," Gillian ordered.

"What?" Perry said.

"Pray for rain. I am not good at sports." Gillian finished with her shoes and then stared at her hand. She was wearing the minister's wife's glove. It had seen better days.

"We're more likely to get snow," the minister joked. "I think we're soon going to see what October is really about."

"Yeah," Gillian muttered. "It's all about sweaters."

Without Greg, the dugout was lackluster. Nobody else seemed to notice. Without Greg, Perry acted cockier, bossier and unbearably annoying.

Lisa watched Gillian.

Why didn't Gillian notice?

They lost 10–1. The guy on first base had a tendency to miss even the simplest ground ball. Gillian wasn't kidding when she said she couldn't play. And Perry could throw from third to first; he just couldn't aim. By the end of the game, he stormed off angrily, leaving Gillian without a ride home.

"Pizza?" Lisa suggested weakly.

The minister was willing—no one else—and in the end even he begged off.

"Guess it's just you and me," Lisa said.

Gillian nodded silently as her eyes followed Perry's car, a fading speck on Elm Street.

"He's just upset," Lisa soothed.

"Right."

This week One Stop Pizza wasn't nearly as packed. Lisa and Gillian found a booth in the back and settled down for their late-night meal. For the first time, Gillian wasn't playing the role of bubbly, crazy coworker and best friend. After they ordered, Lisa waited a moment, and then finally offered, "Go ahead. Get if off your chest."

"Perry's changing!" Gillian burst out. "Oh, I know what you think—what everybody thinks—but he didn't use to be so cold, self-centered. It's his job. It's changing him. And I'm really starting to—"

Lisa didn't say a word. Gillian was turning red, fidgeting and looked like she was ready to run. Then her outburst turned to a whisper, "I'm really starting to hate him."

Wow.

"So," Lisa said carefully, "why don't you break up with him?"

"Because you can only hate somebody if you love them. I read that somewhere and it has played over and over in my mind for the last year. And because every once in a while I see a glimmer of the man he used to be, and I think I'm the only one standing between him and the dark side."

"The dark side?"

"I'm convinced that if I step aside, he'll forget his upbringing, his friends and even God."

"Oh, surely not."

"No, I'm serious. Whatever is at the top of the political ladder he's so busy climbing has become everything to him. I'm not in the way because it sounds good to tell his colleagues that he has a teacher girlfriend."

"You cannot be his conscience," Lisa said. "He has to answer to himself."

"Hey, ladies!" At the worst possible time, Vince Frenci

scooted in next to Gillian. Greg's coworker actually cleaned up pretty well. Lisa had only seen him in his stained Konrad Construction gray-and-white-striped shirt and baggy blue pants. In a red tucked-in shirt and jeans, he looked, well… good.

"I was over there with my little brother and saw you two. So, what's up?" He looked Lisa up and down. "Been playing baseball?"

"Softball."

"I thought the season was over." Vince studied Gillian. "You got a cold?"

"Yes."

Their pizza arrived. Lisa took a piece but Gillian didn't move. She sat there, staring at the pizza in a daze. Even Vince noticed. He shifted uncomfortably. "Am I interrupting something?"

"We were just having a pity party," Gillian sniffed.

Surprised, Lisa took a bite and waited to see what Gillian would do next.

But it wasn't what Gillian said that rocked her world, it was what Vince said. Looking straight at Lisa, he asked, "Are you having trouble with Greg?"

"What?"

"Oh," Vince said airily, "everyone knows something's going on between you two. I've never seen the man so distracted. He used to let that babysitter of his pick Amber up after school, but now the minute school ends, he's gone."

"He's just an overprotective parent, that's all," Lisa protested.

Taking a slice of pizza, Gillian commented, "No, I'm with Vince on this one. I not only *think* he likes you, but I *know* you also like him. Last week, you two were a team all by yourselves. I've never seen anything like it. And the team's never played like that."

"That's right," Vince said. "Greg plays softball. How do I get on the team?"

Between bites, Gillian said, "Come to church."

"Will you be there?"

Gillian paused a moment and then slowly said, "Absolutely."

"I just might do that." Vince nodded before standing. "Ladies, it's been a pleasure, but I think I'll leave you to that pity party and rejoin Jimmy."

"Flirt," Gillian muttered.

Watching him go, Lisa couldn't help but wonder if Vince might just be what Gillian needed. She took back that thought a moment later when Gillian continued, "He may be a flirt, but he's right. Greg Bond is interested in you."

"I wish," Lisa responded. "But trust me, he's interested in his daughter. Period."

"No." Gillian shook her head. "It's not just Greg's coworker. Even Mrs. Henry has noticed. She asked me after school today if Greg was your boyfriend. Last year when Amber was in my class, he often picked her up, but not like now. There's a reason why, and I think it's you."

Finishing her final piece of pizza, Lisa remembered last night, the look he gave her before he disappeared—almost ran—from the auditorium. Then she thought about last Friday—the camaraderie on the field, the touch under the table—and she wished she thought so, too. But, unfortunately, even if there were a spark of interest, an attraction, she could tell that there was something holding him back.

Maybe he still loved his late wife.

"I can see doubt on your face," Gillian observed.

"And I can feel doubt in my heart."

"Let's do something about that!" Gillian exclaimed. "Just

because my love life is about to end unhappily-ever-after is no reason yours shouldn't begin."

"As Amber's teacher, I'd really rather not get involved."

"I hear that unspoken word, *yet.* Okay, I somewhat understand, but there's no reason we can't go over tomorrow, real friendly, since I also attend Greg's church, and take him a basket of food."

"You go. I think it's a good idea."

Smiling for the first time all evening, Gillian said, "Oh, I'm going all right, and if you don't go with me, there's no telling what I just might accidentally say to him."

"Why didn't you tell me when you noticed the first spot?" By Greg's count, yesterday when he'd kept Amber home from school, the number of spots had climbed to more than two hundred. Today, there seemed to be even more. According to the Internet, the number could climb to the thousands. Luckily, there was no need to call a doctor unless Amber's fever hit 104 degrees. To Greg's shame the Internet also mentioned that chicken pox, as a childhood disease, had almost disappeared. Seemed most kids were vaccinated.

If Rachel were alive, Amber would keep regular doctor's appointments.

"I didn't know what they were, Daddy. I thought they were bug bites."

Looking at his watch, Greg could only shake his head. Burt was due any minute, taking Amber to the babysitter was out of the question, and Greg's biggest worry was that Amber would overhear something. He still hadn't figured out what to do when, ten minutes later, the doorbell rang.

Burt was early.

Peeking out the window, he wished it was an early Burt. On

his doorstep stood Gillian with a casserole dish and Lisa with a grocery sack. A bag of potato chips stuck out of the top, alongside a coloring book.

Great, just great. No way could he pretend he wasn't home.

He opened the door. "Hello, ladies. Been shopping?"

"We thought you might need food," Gillian said.

Greg looked at Lisa. She didn't say a word. This whole adventure was probably Gillian's idea. Lisa didn't strike him as forward enough. She was more subtle. She'd win a guy over with a gentle touch on the arm, a knee pressed against his and a smile.

Still, here she stood on his porch, looking like she belonged next to Amber's bike, as if she hadn't minded stepping over chalk marks on the sidewalk, and as if she didn't really object to Gillian teaching her about the time-honored casserole brigade.

Truth: he did need food. Bigger truth: he had to get Lisa and Gillian out of here before Burt arrived. Reality: Burt's car was just now pulling up behind Gillian's.

This is not what he needed today. Thinking quickly, he reached for the grocery bag. "I cannot tell you how much I appreciate this. We were getting low, and I know Amber will be excited that her two favorite teachers stopped by."

Burt paused on the sidewalk and hesitated a second too long. Both ladies looked.

Greg didn't need for Gillian and Lisa to expect an introduction—he needed to keep them out of this—but what else could he do?

It was his fault. He shouldn't have joined the softball team; he should have homeschooled Amber; he should have—

"Mr. Bond," Burt said smoothly when he reached them. "I'm Burt Kelley, representing System Health Insurance. Am I on time?"

Real name, fake job—Greg wished his own life were as easy. "Right on time," he said. "Did you get my message about my daughter having the chicken pox?"

"I did. I had them as a child." He nodded at Gillian and Lisa, then said, "Ladies," and after adjusting his hold on his briefcase, he relieved Gillian of the casserole.

Greg clutched the grocery bag he'd taken from Lisa and moved aside to let Burt enter. Then he addressed the two women. "The house is a mess, as you can see I also have a meeting with Mr. Kelley and, quite frankly, Amber's not feeling well. As much as I appreciate the visit, today's not the day."

"But—" Gillian began.

"We understand," Lisa interrupted. She tugged on Gillian's arm. "Call us if you need anything else."

"I will," he promised. Then he watched as they headed down the front walk to Gillian's car. Gillian scooted, ever the energetic one, while Lisa seemed to glide. As Lisa got in the car, she looked at him.

These long looks had to stop. He was pulling her into danger.

After Gillian's car drove off, Greg led Burt to the kitchen. "Nice save, pretending to be an insurance salesman. They're from Amber's school. Gillian also attends my church."

"I think it was the ladies at my neighborhood church who first inspired me to attend, too," Burt joked.

"Oh, it's not the ladies who get me in the door," Greg contradicted.

"Then what? When you first started going, I was happy. It was one of the first of my brilliant suggestions that you actually followed. Still, attending church? It's so the opposite of who you were back in Wellington. I thought it added to your new identity, but now you're buying into it, aren't you?"

"Completely."

"So, do you now think that if you were a believer back in Wellington, that Rachel might still be alive?"

Greg was quiet. For a while, when he'd first started reading his Bible and listening to the Word, he'd fought that very thought. It only added to his guilt. Truth was, he didn't believe that *not* belonging to the church had anything to do with the way things had turned out. What he'd learned, though, was that having God to lean on made just about any situation bearable.

His biggest regret was that Rachel, his darling Rachel, had never been introduced to the Bible. He also regretted that he'd not answered the door to God's knocking back when he was a foster kid and had actually landed in a home with a decent family. He needed God now, and he knew it. But he'd needed God then and by not knowing it, not accepting it, he'd struggled alone for far too long.

"We have a bit of a problem," Greg finally said. "I can't take Amber to the babysitter. We're going to need to be careful how loudly we talk."

Burt sobered. "I've got quite a bit to say."

The new coloring book from Miss Jacoby took Amber's mind off her itching, somewhat. It didn't stop her from itching, just took away the grimace while she was doing it. As Greg dished out noodle casserole and a drink for Amber, leaving her to color and nibble on her food, he also made plates for him and Burt and took them into his office.

A minute later, Burt emptied the contents of his briefcase onto Greg's desk. There were yearbooks for all four years Rachel had attended Valley High. There were statements from her close friends, copies of all the blog comments as well as newspaper reports and even video of newscasts. Burt had copies of police reports with sticky notes posted wherever he had a question.

"Before we start going through this stuff, let me tell you what happened in Lawrence."

He started with the main library, a building Greg had seen but never visited. "It was cold, and fairly crowded."

"There's not much to do in Lawrence, Kansas," Greg muttered.

"Maybe that's why the librarians didn't flinch when I asked them questions. They didn't ask for identification, either. Not on Friday. When I went back on Saturday, Shelly Mosar, the head librarian brought up my Web site. She'd apparently had second thoughts about assisting me."

"I'd have second thoughts after seeing your Web site, too," Greg said.

"Hey, it's functional. It's not like I can show my client list. And it did convince Shelly to tell me even more."

"Why's that?"

"She noticed I was from Littletree, Missouri."

"Same as me?"

"Same as you. She attended your wedding. Seems she thinks you're innocent, so you have one more person who believes in you."

Suddenly, Greg understood a parable that had always escaped him. The parable of the lost sheep.

The importance of one.

EIGHT

More than two hundred people had attended the Cooke/Travis wedding. One hundred and ninety were from Rachel's side. Five were Alex/Greg's friends from college. Five—probably more—were crashers. There wasn't a chance Greg would remember the librarian. "Great, so how did this help us?"

"I spent more than an hour at the library, going through old newspapers and other records. I discovered a few things, as you'll soon see. First I have a list of everyone who used the computers on the day someone posted, 'You can run but you can't hide. You're the reason your wife died.' The librarian even gave me who the repeat users were and who the first-time users were."

"Anyone of interest?"

"I think so, and you're going to help me narrow down the field." Burt nodded toward the stuff he'd emptied from his briefcase. "The second thing I discovered when I went to Lawrence High. All the yearbooks from Rachel's years are missing."

"What did the librarian say about that?"

"This was the school librarian, not as helpful as the public librarian. She said they've been missing for about two years."

"The librarian have any ideas?"

"No, and until I stopped by, she didn't think much of it. Seems things like yearbooks go missing all the time. She blames kids and parents who don't want to pay the high price."

Greg looked at the table. Four yearbooks were sitting there. "So, then, how did you get the yearbooks?"

"A few of Rachel's friends still live in Lawrence. I heard all about her days as a cheerleader. The class president is still in town. He's a banker like you. You didn't tell me Rachel was an honors student. One of her Advanced Placement English buddies handed over her yearbooks when I told her it might help bring Rachel's killer to justice."

"Was the librarian the only one who thinks I'm innocent?"

"They all watch television. The grub mask coming off and someone who looks like you looking into a camera is a bit hard to swallow."

"Tell me about it," Greg muttered.

"I didn't tell them I worked for you, and because I'm a bail bondsman, it kind of leads them to believe I'm looking for you. While I was at Lawrence High, I visited some of Rachel's teachers. A couple looked at my list of computer users. The only thing I asked was if Rachel might have known any of them."

"And?"

"I got five names."

Five names! It was more than they'd had in the last six months.

"Go on," Greg urged.

"I also went to the flower shop Rachel worked at during high school. No one remembered her—but I come to find out it's changed owners about four times."

"Tell me about the five names."

"No, first I want you to go through these yearbooks. Write down every name that you think might have a connection with Rachel. You can look at my interview notes. I want friends, enemies and even someone who might have worshiped your wife from afar."

"But—"

"It will save time in the long run. I've got a list of five. If you give me a list, and we see someone whose name appears on both lists, we know where to start."

First Greg looked at the yearbooks, matched interviews to Rachel's friends and pointed out five friends Burt had missed.

Burt, ever the professional, pointed to two sisters. "They no longer live in Lawrence or close by." He pointed to another picture. "He's a missionary, serving in Africa."

Greg almost dropped the yearbook. Burt never asked, and Greg had never volunteered, but the money he was paying Burt couldn't be earned by a construction worker, and there wasn't a chance Greg could be using *his* own money, money he'd had before his arrest, since the authorities had frozen his bank accounts.

No, Greg's construction-worker salary paid the rent on the simple three-bedroom house and provided for food and a few extras—nothing more.

Quite a difference compared to his bank manager's salary, which had allowed his family to live in a beautiful five-bedroom house and had let them acquire any extras they might have wanted.

Greg Bond—the real Greg Bond—was a customer of the Wellington Bank. He was a multimillionaire, not that you'd know it by looking at him. He had a trust fund, invested well, and kept a very healthy bank account.

He was also a missionary in Africa who hadn't returned to the States in years. Occasionally, he used his own money, but in all the years he had banked with Wellington Bank, he'd been more or less an eccentric.

Alex Cooke had started his banking career as a teller. Greg

Bond had been the first bank customer Alex struck up an acquaintance with.

Then, as Alex advanced professionally, the real Greg—who invested wisely—more than once used him as a liaison. The result was a working relationship that meant that Alex knew Greg Bond's social security number by heart. He knew how to navigate the man's money market account. And Alex also knew what Greg's signature looked like.

It hadn't taken much effort to adopt Greg's identity. It took more effort to keep the guilt at bay. And since becoming a Christian, guilt took on a whole new meaning. That Alex intended to pay back every dime wasn't much comfort.

"This classmate is dead," Burt said, bringing Greg back to the present. "And this one is in a wheelchair."

Burt slowly closed the yearbook, keeping one finger marking Annie's page. "Reunion? You brought that up once before. I should have jumped on it. When, exactly, was this reunion?"

"It was almost two years ago. Rachel's tenth. We went back to Lawrence for the weekend. I didn't think it was important."

"Everything having to do with you and Rachel is important." Burt thrust the yearbook at him. "Go through it now, again." Stern didn't begin to describe his tone. "I put a sticky note by everyone I determined was an acquaintance of Rachel's. Now, I want everyone who came to that reunion, who spoke with Rachel, who so much as waved at you or Rachel. Then I'll show you my list of five."

Greg felt a wild urge to apologize. He suppressed it. Every fiber of his being seemed to come to life. In the last six months, at least before Rachel's body turned up, it seemed as if Burt's investigation had hit its final dead end. With Rachel surfacing, a door of opportunity opened, one that offered Greg a chance of redemption.

Who knew how long the door would remain open?

Burt took over Greg's desk. He had the screen advertising Rachel's ten-year reunion up in a matter of minutes. While he navigated the site, he made phone calls on his cell.

Greg turned his attention to the yearbook, Rachel's graduation year. In just twenty minutes, he had fifteen names. A few he remembered from the wedding. A few more he remembered from the reunion. He had the bridesmaids. He had a girl who'd dropped out of school during their junior year, but she'd come to the reunion. Who knows why Greg remembered her? He had the boy who worked at the flower shop where Rachel had worked. He had the girl who worked at the burger place Rachel and her friends had gone to after school. He had the brother of one of her classmates, and he had three people who'd been in various plays with Rachel.

Burt all but snatched the list. "Fifteen. I expected more." He was quiet for a moment, silently counting. "Three are the same. I'll start with them."

"Let me see the list." Greg snatched it the minute Burt took it from his pocket.

Dan Anderson
Robert Thomas
Diego Gonzales
Anthony Buckman
Christopher Engstrom

"The librarian eliminated all the teenagers and all the females," Burt said. "Tell me about these three. Tell me about Robert Thomas, Diego Gonzales and Anthony Buckman."

Burt had been right to force Greg to go over interviews, newspaper reports and other materials. Names and faces were somewhat fresh in his mind. "Lisa introduced me to Robert at the reunion. He was an honors student. They were in some club together. He's something of a nerd. He lives in California now. Not married. He didn't come to our wedding. Diego delivered flowers for the florist where she worked. He joined the military after high school. He lives in Hawaii, I think. I remember Rachel was surprised that he came to the wedding. He was at the reunion. Not married. He also doesn't look anything like me. He's about a foot taller, a hundred pounds heavier and speaks with an accent."

"He was all those things two years ago at the reunion. A lot can change in a year. I'll put him down to third on the list, but I'm not discounting him."

Greg almost said, "How do you change skin tone?" but then he remembered the makeup. Still, Diego seemed like a long shot.

"Now tell me about Anthony," Burt ordered.

"Anthony was a football player. I think I've heard about him the most. She dated him for a while during her senior year. She always teased me that I should be jealous."

"Were you?"

"What, jealous? Nah. He came to our wedding. Early twenties and he was already on wife number two. Rachel truly considered herself blessed to have me." Greg shook his head. *Blessed* had been her word, not his. Now that he knew the true meaning of *blessed,* he was humbled. "Maybe if she'd married one of the other guys, she'd still be alive."

"And then Amber wouldn't exist," Burt said calmly.

Greg stood. Every day he thanked God for Amber's existence. It was past time to check on her.

She was asleep, her head—dark hair fanning out—draped over the coloring book and a red crayon in her dangling hand. Her food was virtually untouched. No surprise. Everything he read said the chicken pox pretty much destroyed the appetite.

He carried her to her room. It was half the size of her old room, and he could count the number of toys she owned on both hands.

After tucking her in, he headed back to his office, to Burt, and to what he hoped was the beginning of the end.

Burt was more than ready to get back to work. He leaned forward, shaking the list of names. "Now that we have these names, why don't we look over the blog comments? See if you can recognize the language, style, maybe a catchphrase of someone you and Rachel knew—especially these three?"

"I've read them a hundred times since they've been posted. There's nothing. Besides, I didn't know these people— Rachel did."

Burt's cell phone rang. He put the caller on hold and pointed to the newspaper articles and the police reports. "Read these. See if anything jumps out at you. You're looking for anything that doesn't add up."

"I've read all these newspaper accounts. I've already told you what jumped out at me. While you're investigating these guys, look for a theater connection. My guess is I'm-on-my-third-wife-and-played-football-in-high-school wouldn't be opposed to playing a leading man."

Burt looked annoyed as he said into the phone, "Yes, I've got three names. I need to find out if they have criminal records."

Thursday morning it snowed. Sherman took on the look of surprised quaintness as Greg chauffeured Amber to school. He was exhausted, physically and mentally. On the one hand, he knew—just knew—they were close to finding the killer. On the other hand, justice was exacting a heavy price. He took a breath, said a prayer and pushed aside his worries *for now*. No need for Amber to pick up on his mood. She already knew something was going on. She'd been looking at her mother's yearbooks and asking questions. Luckily, the questions were harmless, like "If I were a cheerleader like Mom, would I get to wear a short skirt?"

No. The more single parenting Greg did, and the more he saw how some of the fifth- and sixth-grade girls dressed, the more he supported a 1950s dress code.

Or, "Why is Mom washing cars?"

Cheerleaders always participated in fund-raisers—school spirit and all that. That was actually how he met Rachel. Her school spirit continued into college, when she'd been collecting signatures on a petition. He didn't even remember what the petition was for. He'd signed away his heart.

And one last question, "Was Mom in all the school plays?"

Greg didn't know. But it didn't matter because before he could formulate an answer, Amber was already onto a different subject.

"I hope Tiffany doesn't get the chicken pox. Because of the snow, we'll have to play in the gym. It's boring if she's not there," Amber said. Then she took off her red mittens again. She'd spent the whole drive taking them off and putting them back on. Her best argument had been, "But Daddy, you don't wear gloves."

He didn't. During most of his foster care years, something as trivial as gloves didn't seem to make it to his caregivers' thoughts.

But gloves weren't trivial when it was his daughter who might have cold fingers. "They're not doing their job if you keep taking them off," he advised. Not that Amber really needed the mittens. This first snowfall was nothing. The only surprise was that it had come so early. Greg couldn't remember the last time October brought anything but a light dusting. It would be gone by evening.

"Mom had mittens like this," Amber said quietly. "I saw them in a picture in her yearbook."

He had no response. For one, he didn't remember if Rachel had red mittens or not. He wished he could. Sometimes he thought he was so busy searching his memory for any clue as to why she was murdered that he was forgetting the little everyday memories.

Him and Rachel in the front yard, playing keep-away from Amber, and getting wet when the sprinklers unexpectedly came on.

Him and Rachel arguing over her wish to go bike riding *as a family* and him saying *Too tired.*

Him and Rachel on the couch after Amber had gone to bed, talking about going on vacation. She wanted to go to Disneyland; he wanted to play golf.

He wished all his memories were like the first one: them together as a family.

Well, one thing was for sure—he was a family man now. He rode bikes with Amber, and he understood the desire for a family-oriented vacation. He also was the primary chauffeur. As Amber climbed out of the car, he noticed that the kids of Sherman Elementary were already celebrating the snowstorm—making snow angels, throwing snowballs and simply jumping in the snow and making a mess.

"Don't even think it," he warned Amber.

"But—"

"You've been sick."

He escorted Amber to the gym, helped her take off her boots, and then left her there while he went to her classroom. She probably had a whole stack of make-up work.

Lisa Jacoby sat at her desk, head bent, writing something on a piece of paper. The room was decorated for fall—scarecrows and pumpkins amid a sea of trees losing their leaves. Lisa was dressed in the same motif: she had an orange bow in her red hair and was wearing an orange sweater with smiling scarecrows. As she scribbled on a piece of paper, the tip of her tongue peeked out.

"Ahem." It came out more gruffly than he'd meant for it to.

She lit up, and he wondered what she'd look like at Christmas. Just as quickly, she blushed. "Mr. Bond! I take it Amber's back today."

She stood and now he could see the yellow satiny shirt she wore under the sweater. She came around the desk. Her brown pants were the only ho-hum item she wore. Even her shoes were orange.

Amber would want a pair now.

"She's feeling much better. I thought I'd stop by and get her work so nothing gets lost."

It only took a moment, and soon Lisa was handing him a folder. His fingers slid across hers and it was all he could do not to jump back.

Really, a woman's touch should not have this effect. He might be single but he wasn't free.

Amber's name was written neatly at the top and a We Missed You sticker was next to it.

Greg needed to get moving. "Any special instructions?"

"No, not really. Read her the directions and she'll know what to do. Amber's actually working well ahead of her peers. She's in the top reading group, and she's already earned five addition stickers."

Reading didn't surprise him. They read almost every night. Math, well, she came by that naturally.

Still, the information gave him pause. It was Amber's happiness at school that made him hesitate about running. And, truthfully, he didn't want to leave. He had friends and running, right now, would only take away time that he could use following up on Rachel's class reunion.

He asked anyway, "If she missed more school, say, I had to move and I didn't put her in the new school until January, would it hurt her much?"

"Any time away from the classroom is lost time, Mr. Bond. Are you moving?"

He almost wished he hadn't asked because now he needed to explain. Then again, since he knew Lisa felt the attraction, too, it was a wise move. If she thought he'd only be in town two or three more months, then maybe she'd distance herself. "I'm not sure. Something's come up and I might have to grab an opportunity."

"Well," she said slowly. "The softball team will miss you."

Yeah, he'd miss the softball team, too, especially the personality on second base.

He backed out of the room before he had time to analyze whether her eyes had darkened. Female emotions had always stumped him, and little Miss Innocent wore her heart on her sleeve.

Come to think of it, so did Amber. He stopped by the gym and watched her happily chasing Mikey Maxwell. Yup, his little girl wasn't shy. She'd catch her man.

She'd miss Mikey almost as much as he'd miss…

No one, he told himself. *He'd miss no one.*

Stepping outside, he headed for his truck. He needed to get to work. He'd be the gopher for Vince, anything Vince needed—hauling material, setting up containment rooms or general cleaning.

It was grunt work, and it gave Greg plenty of time to think. Since Saturday, he'd typed every single name from Rachel's yearbook into the computer searching engine, looking for Web sites, looking for blogs, looking for anything. He'd especially looked for instances where Rachel's name appeared with either Robert, Diego or Tony.

Tony showed up the most.

He'd found pictures, lots from the reunion. He'd printed them out and if he could, he'd named everyone he recognized who had come in contact with Rachel. He'd forgotten to add teachers to his original list.

According to Burt, the police had already taken whatever they wanted from the house as evidence. Then the bank—Greg's bank—had taken the house and auctioned off the contents. Rachel's real yearbooks—the ones with her friends' signatures—where were they? Did the police have them? Did the police also have the family photos? Had some stranger bought them?

Or did the murderer have them?

NINE

The snow melted; the mud stayed. Lisa loved it. Tucson seldom—and never in Lisa's memory—got snow.

Growing up, Lisa thought snow meant the world had come to a standstill. Not in Sherman and certainly not during the final game of the season. The minister insisted that the show must go on, even if he wound up a little shorthanded. This Friday, Mikey's mother had a cold and one of the outfielders had to work. They were the only ones they knew for sure wouldn't be there. Perry took first base; Lisa had second. Gillian, complaining every step of the way, was in the outfield.

It was almost too cold to warm up. Gillian stood next to Lisa as Perry practiced throwing from first to second.

"If Greg doesn't show up, I am not playing third," Gillian groused, watching Lisa catch.

"The minister would move shortstop to third and do without a shortstop before he'd ask you to do that," Lisa assured, tossing the ball back to Perry.

"How come you're not assuring me that Greg will show up?"

"Because I don't know if Greg will show up or not." It took all of Lisa's willpower not to check the parking lot again while Perry chased the ball. She'd already checked about twenty times. She also scanned the park. Except for the softball game, it was pretty empty. Gone were the skateboarders and bicyclists. There were a few families scattered about. One tried to make a snowman out of mud and snow. Another played a game of tag. A couple sat on a bench snuggling. A lone man leaned against a tree. Funny, with the park nearly empty, Lisa had the strangest feeling that she was being watched.

"Surely Greg'd call if he weren't going to show," Gillian said about the time Perry returned to first base.

Until yesterday, Lisa would have believed that, too, but he'd surprised her. He might move? Keep Amber out of school for months? Where was this coming from?

"I think he'd call," Lisa finally agreed as the players moved to the dugout. "Hey, did he ever say anything to you last year about possibly moving?"

"They came well after Christmas," Gillian said. "For the first two months Amber would pack all her belongings into her backpack at the end of the school day. It's one thing you learn, teaching school, your attendance chart on Friday might not be the same as your attendance chart come Monday. After a while, I spoke to her father about it, and then it stopped."

"You never told me about that."

"Quite honestly, I forgot." Gillian patted Lisa's arm. "By the way, you can stop checking the parking lot. He's here."

Well, Amber certainly didn't act as if anything were amiss. She managed to sprint from the brown pickup in record time, skipped in front of her father, mindless of the mud, and then crossed her arms and pouted right when she got to the dugout. "Where's Mikey?"

"His mother has a cold," Lisa said.

"So does my daddy and he's still going to play."

Behind Amber, Greg shook his head. "It's nothing. I sneezed

twice on the way over. I'm pretty sure I'm allergic to Amber's Hannah Montana CD."

"That'll do it," the minister said before calling out the next three batters. Greg went second. Lisa third.

Greg's mind obviously wasn't on the game. He struck out. When Lisa slid—playing softball in melting snow was a real challenge—into first base, she watched as he made sure Amber was bundled and sitting tight on the bleachers. Tiffany must be home with Mom because not a single kid, besides Amber, made it to the game.

Maybe that's why Greg was distracted. No babysitter. A moment later, as Lisa grabbed her glove and headed for second base, she noticed Greg looking toward the family playing tag. He looked spooked, too.

The couple was gone, as was the lone man. Only the families remained.

She heard the crack of a bat hitting a ball just in time to see it heading her way. She dove, missed and went down hard in the cold, cold, dirt. Gillian limply chased it to the back fence, and a player who didn't deserve a home run got one.

"You okay?" Greg asked, helping Lisa up.

"Fine."

"Guess in sunny Arizona there wasn't much chance to play in this type of weather?"

"No, but that's not my problem."

"Then what is?"

"Nothing," she responded, because she couldn't very well say *You*.

They lost the game 5–3, season over. They didn't make it to the playoffs. Lisa was pretty amazed that the team still considered their trip to the pizza place a celebration.

Whether it was Gillian's finagling or just plain luck, Lisa

wound up next to Greg with Gillian on her other side. He, of course, acted like she was just anybody. He offered her a slice of pizza. Passed her tea to the waitress for a refill. Offered her a second slice of pizza. And basically, did not do one single thing as exciting as touching her leg.

Amber, somewhat bored without either Tiffany or Mikey, ate two pieces of pizza—sausage still intact—and colored four place mats.

"We came in fifth," the minister gloated. "Fifth. The best we've ever done."

"I enjoyed playing first base," Perry said. "Maybe next year we can do some repositioning."

The minister's eyes brightened. He looked at Lisa. "You interested in playing second again?"

"When does the season start?"

"We start practicing late April, early May, depending on the weather, and then the season officially begins in June."

June seemed like eons away. She hadn't really considered her summer schedule. Would she teach summer school? Go home to Tucson? Find a temporary job?

"What do you do in the summer?" she asked Gillian.

"Well, I don't play softball. That's for sure." Gillian looked at Perry. He hadn't taken her ineptness in the outfield quietly. Lisa hadn't heard the murmured words, but she'd seen his facial expression and then she'd seen Gillian's. "I usually work at the church camp."

"I know a guy who is interested in joining our team," Lisa said. "He works with Greg. His name is Vince Frenci."

"When did you talk to Vince?" Greg asked, sounding surprised.

"Last week. He was here at the pizza place. Gillian and I

stopped by after the game. It was pretty deserted. He sat with us for a while."

Perry glared at Gillian. "The Frencis cause a lot of problems in Sherman. They always have, they always will. It's best to avoid them."

"Perry," the minister said. "Do you know Vince Frenci personally?"

"No," Perry admitted. "He was a few years ahead of me in school. But I've dealt with complaints issued against his uncle. The whole family is bad news."

Greg slapped a hand down on the table so hard that Lisa jumped. Amber scolded, "Daddy!"

"I work with Vince," Greg said. "He's never done one thing to make me think he's anything but decent and hardworking. As a matter of fact, I trust him more than I trust you."

"It's late. It's cold." Perry took one last bite of pizza and stood. "Plus, I have to drive into Lincoln tomorrow. I'm leaving before I say anything unfortunate."

It was on the tip of Lisa's tongue to tell him that he already had.

Perry held out his hand to Gillian. "Come on."

"I'm not done with my pizza."

A look of disbelief crossed Perry's face. Lisa could see anger and uncertainty follow. Finally, he said, "Fine."

And he left.

"I'll give you a ride home," Lisa offered.

The minister reached across the table and patted Gillian's hand. "I'll give him a call. Talk to him. It's tough to be a small-town boy in a big politician's world."

Greg cleared his throat. "It's also hard when you're climbing the work ladder and you're giving more attention to your job than your life." He played with his glass of iced tea. "It makes you do and say things you don't really mean."

Lisa couldn't stop looking at Greg. He'd stood up to Perry. He'd defended a friend, an underdog. And when all was said and done, and when Greg rightly had reason to gloat, instead he put himself in the other person's shoes.

Impressive.

The minister was nodding.

Only Gillian seemed unconvinced. Lisa put her arm around her friend but couldn't think of anything to say.

"He didn't even chip in for the pizza," Gillian muttered finally.

It really wasn't funny. Gillian was hurting, and the comment wasn't meant to be funny. But Lisa could see Greg fighting a grin. Even the minister looked as if he wanted to laugh.

"Oh," Gillian said finally. "Go ahead and laugh."

"It's the perfect way to end our get-together," the minister said. "Now I'll be in a much better mood for my evening prayers."

"Where Perry will be mentioned more than once, I hope," Gillian said. "I know God's going to be getting an earful from me."

"I'll pray, too," Greg promised. "I know some of what he's going through."

Then the three of them looked at Lisa.

"Ah, outside of the prayers you guys offer for the pizza, I don't think I've ever said a prayer."

"Well, it's time you learned how," the preacher said.

"I didn't know how to pray, either," Greg confided. "Until moving to Sherman, I'd rarely stepped inside a church and most of my prayers were forced."

"Forced?" the minister asked.

"One of my foster families was religious. Prayers were mandatory. I was too young to appreciate the power of prayer and too angry to care," Greg admitted.

"I don't know you lived in foster care," Gillian said. She no longer looked mad. As easily as that, Gillian went from worrying about herself to worrying about others.

Watching the people who were not only her friends, but also as close to family as she had in Sherman, Lisa suddenly realized that without the weekly softball games, she'd be a bit lonely, a bit disconnected.

"I'll pray, too," she offered.

"Come to church on Sunday," the minister said, "and we'll teach you just how wonderful prayer can be."

"Thanks for the invitation, but I'm leaving in the morning for Omaha. My friend Janni is getting married soon and tomorrow is her wedding shower. I won't be back until Sunday evening."

"Next Sunday, then," the minister suggested.

"Yes," Amber said. "Come to church on Sunday. You can sit with us. You can even color with me."

Greg looked trapped.

Omaha had, at one time, been the capital of Nebraska. If size mattered, Omaha should still be the capital. Maybe it came from three months living in a small town where every convenience was merely twenty minutes from home that got Lisa turned around.

Or maybe it was that her mind was simply elsewhere.

The four hours it took to drive from Sherman to Omaha were spent thinking about Greg Bond, the fact that he might be moving and the fact that he'd definitely looked uncomfortable about her attending his church.

Why?

Gillian, of course, had the answer and was more than willing to tell her on the way home.

"It's not that he doesn't want you in church," Gillian had said. "It's more that he's afraid he *does* want you in church and probably a few other places, too."

"Gillian!" Lisa's gasp had been enough to momentarily stop Gillian from saying anything else, but Lisa knew she hadn't heard the end of it.

These thoughts and more were responsible for two wrong turns and one sniffly meltdown. Lisa arrived at the shower thirty minutes late and could only blame the unexpected scenic route.

She didn't need to blame anything. No one seemed to notice that she was late. Six of her best college friends, from four different states, squealed when she arrived, and in a matter of minutes, it was life back in the dorm all over again.

The shower lasted two hours; afterward the friends went out for dinner. Lisa didn't drive; no telling where they'd wind up if she had. Then it was back to Janni's house for a sleepover. They watched a romantic comedy and caught up on life after college. Just before ten, Lisa and Janni ran to the neighborhood superstore. Their mission: more snacks and a just-released movie. Once inside, Janni proved that Omaha wasn't nearly as big as Lisa had thought. Three people stopped them and talked wedding plans. Even the cashier knew Janni by name.

As they left the store, someone else hollered, "Janni!"

Lisa leaned against the shopping cart while Janni hurried back to talk to a white-haired woman.

It might be midnight before they got back to Janni's house.

Shifting, Lisa moved to lean against the wall. The wall that held the flyers advertising missing children. Studying the photos, she couldn't even fathom losing a child. During recess, she was constantly counting and recounting her students.

Especially little Amber Bond, whose daddy was so overprotective.

Little Amber Bond, whose exact likeness—a little girl named Amy Cooke—was staring at Lisa from a missing/endangered child poster.

TEN

"What's wrong with you?" Janni asked.

Lisa jumped. She hadn't even heard Janni walk up. Opening her mouth, Lisa tried to think of something to say, something to do. She couldn't, so she closed her mouth and waited for the sky to fall. When it didn't, she looked at the poster again.

No, it couldn't be. If it hadn't been for the school play, in which Amber had worn a blond wig she'd never have looked twice at the blond child—same smile; Amber's smile—looking at the world from a missing child poster.

"Lisa, you're scaring me. What's wrong?"

"Nothing. Nothing's wrong," Lisa stammered. "I think the long drive, getting lost, the excitement, everything, just finally hit me."

Tell her!

Tell Janni what? That the little girl on the poster resembled one of her students? And that the Greg Bond Lisa had mentioned over dinner fleetingly—but not fleetingly enough, because the girls had all figured out that Lisa was more than interested—might be a kidnapper?

No, not a chance. The little girl just happened to look like Amber. Similar, not the same. Lisa looked again.

And wasn't convinced.

One thing for sure, mentioning her fears to Janni would put a damper on the wedding shower and change the focus of the night.

But if Amber truly were Amy, it needed to be done.

Now.

"Janni, I need to make a phone call."

"Are you sick? You look so funny."

"I'm not sick. I, I just need to make a phone call."

"Lisa, you're scaring me," Janni said.

What Lisa wanted to do was shout that she did indeed feel funny, scared and ready to faint. What she didn't want to do was ruin Janni's party. Besides, the picture couldn't possibly be Amber Bond.

Lisa looked at the picture again.

It *was* Amber Bond. Dread curled in her stomach until every skin cell, every nerve ending, every part of Lisa Jacoby felt like it was *crawling.*

A strength she didn't know she possessed surfaced. She forced her lips into a stiff smile and said, "It's just that I forgot to do something, and a quick call will remedy everything. Why don't you go ahead to the car."

Janni walked away, mumbling about knowing something was wrong, all the while looking back occasionally and shaking her head. Lisa, hand trembling, took out her cell phone and punched in Gillian's number. Never mind that it was eleven at night. Never mind that Gillian lived with her parents. Before Lisa called the number from the missing child poster, she was making sure—*sure of what, she didn't quite know*—and the only person who might be able to giver her advice was Gillian.

Gillian's dad answered.

Great, if she sounded upset, he'd want to know why. If she didn't sound upset, he'd want to know why she'd awakened the family.

She opted for the upset. There wasn't really a choice, as Lisa was back staring at the missing child's poster and looking at a likeness that had to be, *had to be,* Amber Bond. After a minute, a very groggy Gillian was on the line.

"Listen," Lisa hissed before Gillian had time to do anything but say, "Hello." "I'm at a store in Omaha, and there are posters of missing children on the wall. One of them is Amber Bond."

There was a second of silence, and then Gillian said, "No way."

"Yes way. Only her name isn't Amber Bond on the missing poster. It's Amy Cooke, and she's a blond. You remember she was supposed to play the teacher in the Open House play. Well, I had her in a blond wig. It's her. Spitting image. I almost fell over when I saw the poster."

Gillian was silent for a moment. "And you're 100 percent sure?"

"No, if I were 100 percent sure, I would have already called the hotline number."

"Tell me what the poster says," Gillian demanded. "Every word!"

"Amy Loretta Cooke, born Feb. 10, just six years ago." Lisa's words were stumbling out one after the other, choppy. She could hear each word getting louder as her fear magnified. "She went missing last year on August 18 from Wellington, Kansas."

A shopper paused, staring at Lisa. It was enough to convince Lisa to rein herself in, slow down, calm down and talk in a hushed voice. "She's white, blond with blue eyes. She's three-foot-five and weighs forty-two pounds. Age today would be six. Circumstances: Amy was abducted by her father, Alex Cooke, on January 18 of this year. An FBI warrant for kidnapping was issued for the abductor on February 5, 2008. They were last seen in a stolen bright blue Dodge van. Caution is advised."

Then Lisa's eyes traveled to the bottom of the poster. "Wait!

There's more. There's a picture of Alex Cooke at the bottom. He's also missing from Wellington, Kansas, same day as Amy. He'd be thirty-three now."

"Does it look like Greg?" Gillian wanted to know.

Lisa finally let go of the death grip she had on the phone. She also remembered to breathe. "No. Alex Cooke is slender, very white collar with short, trendy brown hair and a little goatee."

Greg Bond was a laborer, rock hard and solid, nothing white collar about him. His black hair needing cutting and he made stubble look good. He had the most amazing blue eyes.

"Well, there you have it," Gillian soothed. "Nothing to worry about. It's just a case of two kids looking alike."

"No," Lisa insisted. "I'm standing here in front of the poster and I'm telling you, I'm looking at Amber, and all I can think about is you telling me how Amber packed up her belongings every day. Plus, every time I'm with Greg, if he's not keeping an eagle eye on Amber, he's checking out the street. Have you ever noticed that?"

"Sure, my grandfather does the same thing. He blames the habit on the war. I'm not sure which one. Come on, Lisa, does Greg strike you as someone who would kidnap his own child?"

It took Lisa a moment to swallow her fear. "He strikes me as a loving father. Maybe his wife denied him custody or something."

"Maybe," Gillian said slowly. "Although I doubt it."

"And maybe that wife is heartbroken right now, and doesn't know if her daughter is alive or dead."

"Look, are you staying at a motel?" Gillian demanded.

"No, I'm staying with my friend Janni."

"First, yank that poster from the wall. Bring it with you when you come home tomorrow. And come right to my house. I'm going to do an Internet search on Alex Cooke. I'll even do one on Amy Cooke, find her poster. I'll find out everything I can. If I'm sure that Greg Bond is Alex Cooke, I'll call you tonight on your cell. If I'm not convinced, let's take what we know and make a decision tomorrow."

Lisa nodded first, then squeaked out "Okay."

"You get some sleep," Gillian ordered. "I don't want anything to happen to you while you're driving home to Sherman."

Home to Sherman? How quickly it had become home. How quickly she'd fallen in love with its people.

And how quickly people like Greg Bond and his daughter had become part of the fabric of her life.

Amber went through three outfits before settling on a dress Greg had previously stipulated was only for special occasions.

Even while he remembered making that rule, he calculated how long before she would grow out of the dress. It looked like his daughter was attending church as if she were a flower girl in someone's very pink wedding. Well, at least she'd be warm.

"Maybe Miss Jacoby will be there," Amber argued, not knowing she'd already won.

"Go ahead and wear the dress, and as far as Miss Jacoby, you know she's out of town. She told you she had a wedding shower to attend."

"Did Mom have a wedding shower?"

"She had two. One was held by her friends and family, the other was held by her friends at work."

"I didn't know Mommy worked." Amber bunched up her face. "I don't remember her working."

"She stopped working after you were born. Before you, she worked at a local theater. She handled props, sold tickets, helped with publicity."

"Sounds like fun."

"Your mom liked it."

He'd remembered a lot of the names of people Rachel worked with. Burt found out the rest. There didn't seem to be a connection between the bank robbery, Rachel's murder and her work at the theater. No surprise. She hadn't worked there in five years.

The drive to church was filled with discussions over what might happen in Bible class. Mostly what Tiffany might be wearing—seemed the girls had gotten together and discussed pretending to be fairy princesses—and how Mikey would behave. Amber also wanted to discuss lunch. She wanted spaghetti, again, and Greg almost said no, but then realized that spaghetti two days in a row wasn't much of a hassle, really.

He delivered Amber to Bible class and was surprised to find her teacher already there. Gillian usually hustled in about three minutes late, lesson in hand and a smile on her face.

She wasn't smiling today. She looked exhausted as she placed papers and scissors on the classroom table. Crayons already waited. Amber's eyes lit up.

"Not until class begins," Greg warned.

Gillian looked up, and by the expression on her face, it almost looked as if she'd seen a ghost. She stared, without blinking, her mouth open to a silent O. Before becoming a fugitive, he'd always locked eyes whenever someone dared to scrutinize him. Now stares made him fight the urge to look at the floor, the ceiling, the door and escape. He forced himself to remain calm and asked, "You all right, Miss Magee?"

She had the grace to blush. "I'm fine. I just didn't get much sleep this weekend."

"You still thinking about Perry?"

She nodded.

"You want me to talk to him?"

If anything, the suggestion made her go even redder. "No, this is something I need to deal with myself," she finally said.

He left Amber helping with the crayons, making sure each batch didn't have duplicate colors and no black—seemed, according to Amber, that black went missing the most—and then headed to his own class.

He felt Gillian's gaze all the way down the hall. Lately, he always seemed to have the feeling that he was being watched. He'd mentioned it to Burt when he phoned yesterday. And Burt hadn't been surprised. He'd sounded concerned. He thought they were getting closer. He also still thought Greg should stay put, act normal, be seen.

Nobody else even knew what was happening. Certainly not the cops who wasted their time searching exclusively for Alex Cooke. And Burt insisted that they not go to the cops with their list until they had narrowed it to just one, complete with some evidence.

There were times when Greg wanted to confide in the minister, but to do so might put the man in danger.

Taking a seat at the back of the empty auditorium, he opened his Bible and closed his eyes, glad to find this moment of peace before class started. There was something comforting about taking a moment to commune with God without distraction, without direction and without discussion.

Just over a year ago, back at the bank, he'd felt the same way about getting to work first. There, he'd enjoyed the calm before the day began. He liked going in, doing the security check and then giving the all clear to the employees.

Then he'd been worried about securing both the bank and his employees; he'd never really thought about his own security.

Which is why it was stupid of the police to consider him the bank robber. If he had been the bank robber, he'd have committed the crime early in the morning when he was alone. He'd have made sure he covered his tracks and made sure no one could possibly get hurt or killed. The police claimed that he felt empowered after robbing the bank. They said he'd killed his wife because he felt invincible.

One thing for sure, in his whole life he'd never felt invincible. The closest he'd come was right now, this minute, in a church building, praying to God.

Father, I'm here. Thank You for this day. Thank You for keeping Amber safe. Watch over us, Lord. Be with Burt and the authorities. Let them find the man who killed my wife and killed the security guard, the man who is doing this to me. Please, Lord, forgive me for wanting justice. Justice is Yours.

According to his concordance, the Bible had more than two hundred references to the word justice. His favorite was in *Luke, chapter 18, verse 3:* And there was a widow in that town who kept coming to him with the plea, *"Grant me justice against my adversary."*

Chapter 4 mentioned that the judge she petitioned for justice cared for neither the woman nor her plea, but finally, because she bugged him enough, he said to himself *"...this woman keeps bothering me, I will see she gets justice, so that she won't eventually wear me out with her coming."*

If it worked for a helpless and vulnerable woman during the first century, it might work for Greg during the twenty-first.

After a late evening fielding Janni's probing questions, followed by a miserable night of no sleep, Lisa hit the road at six in the morning.

She'd never been more awake.

She pulled into Sherman just before ten and headed to Gillian's house in time to see the whole family, obviously dressed for church, piling into Gillian's dad's car.

Lisa put her foot on the brake, slowed and pulled to the side of the road. She couldn't very well flag the family down and demand that Gillian come with her.

She could head home, wait for church to go over and then meet up with Gillian. A quick look at her watch nixed that idea. She'd heard Gillian talk about church. Her fellow teacher never missed and fairly bubbled over when she talked about God. Sunday School was from ten to ten forty-five. The regular service was from eleven to noon, supposedly. Gillian also said that if church ever really did end at noon, it would make the front page of the paper.

Lisa couldn't wait almost three hours. It would drive her nuts. Never mind that she hadn't slept, wasn't dressed properly. She needed to see Gillian, know she was there to talk to, and if Lisa saw Greg, too, well, that was good. Maybe she'd realize that the photo wasn't him.

Wasn't Amber.

By the time she got back on the road, the Magees were already out of sight. No problem. Gillian had invited Lisa to church no less than once a week. Lisa knew where the church was. After a short drive Lisa took a space far from the door, left the car and hurried up the stairs to an empty foyer. She'd been to church a few times, with friends, never alone. This was the first time she'd been late. That made it somewhat easier. When she went with friends, they were always on time and the foyer was always bustling with people. Today she wasn't sure if she could smile and greet people as if she were a typical visitor.

She followed the sound of a man's voice to an auditorium. There were perhaps thirty people scattered throughout the room. Reverend Pynchon was up front. He stopped speaking when Lisa poked her head through the doorway.

"Lisa," he boomed. When did he get such a loud voice? It certainly wasn't that loud at softball. "Welcome. Come join us. There's a seat right there in the back, beside Greg."

The deer-in-the-headlights look had never been more evident on Greg's face; nevertheless, he gave a stoic wave and scooted over.

Lisa took her seat next to him and tried not to hyperventilate. Twenty-nine people—three from the softball league—turned and smiled. The one person Lisa didn't see was Gillian.

Greg leaned over and whispered, "She teaches Sunday School. Amber's class."

"Oh, that's right," Lisa whispered back.

Greg plucked a Bible from the book rack and handed it to her. Then he helped her with her coat. She knew she should recoil, something, but instead all she could do was lean toward him, grinning stupidly, and notice how he smelled of Armani. Her sister's boyfriend wore the same scent. How odd? Armani was expensive, not something she would expect from a construction worker.

Not something she would have even thought twice about if she hadn't seen the wanted poster.

Reverend Pynchon repeated the chapter of the Bible he was preaching from, and Lisa understood that he was addressing her. She'd thumbed through a Bible occasionally, at friends' houses and in motel rooms. Greg solved her dilemma by reaching over, taking the Bible from her lap, finding the place and then handing the Bible back to her.

"Thanks."

She didn't hear one word the preacher said, although she did smile, nod and act as if she were looking at the Bible. When Greg turned a page in his Bible, she turned a page in hers.

She didn't think she fooled him.

Was it possible he'd fooled her and everyone else?

Finally, a bell rang, and class ended. Lisa shook hands with strangers, accepted hugs from the softball team—including the preacher, excluding Greg—and finally headed off to find Gillian.

Instead, Amber found Lisa.

"You're here! Wow! Do you like my dress?"

"I love your dress," Lisa answered. For a possibly kidnapped child, Amber didn't act sad, concerned or fidgety. "As a matter of fact," Lisa shared, surprised by how normal she sounded, "I'll be wearing one very much like it in a few months at my friend Janni's wedding."

"My mommy's bridesmaids all wore red. I've seen the picture. What color will you wear?"

"I'll be wearing blue. It's my friend's favorite color. Her name is Janni. What was your mommy's name?"

Talk about timing, Greg arrived at just that moment, put his hand on Amber's shoulder and said, "My late wife's name was Melissa."

Lisa wasn't sure if he were talking to her or Amber as his voice gentled, "We don't talk about her much."

"Hey!" Gillian walked up, looked from Lisa to Amber to Greg, and asked a really dumb question, "Everyone all right?"

No! Lisa wanted to scream; instead, she nodded.

Greg walked away with Amber holding onto his hand and talking excitedly about her teacher being here.

"I don't think it's him," Gillian whispered. "You know, this morning when Greg dropped Amber off for class, he noticed something was bothering me—mainly what *you* tossed in my lap last night. He thought I was still worried about Perry and offered to talk to him. Greg's not a killer. He's a nice guy."

"I know, believe me, I know. I've thought about everything he's done this year, the way he cares for Amber. I've never seen such a doting father. But I keep remembering that Ted Bundy was a nice guy," Lisa muttered, following Gillian back into the auditorium. She grabbed her coat from the back pew and followed Gillian to another section of pews.

"I saw that movie, too," Gillian said. "Bundy's the exception not the rule. Men who kill their wives and rob banks are usually not nice guys."

In unison, both women scanned the rapidly filling church until they found Greg and Amber. Tiffany had settled in next to them, wearing a dress every bit as elaborate as Amber's—and already both girls were giggling. When they noticed Lisa looking, they giggled even more. Greg glanced their way, his look clearly said *Don't entice them.*

Them being the girls.

"I was up all night," Gillian whispered. "Twice my dad knocked on the door and asked me what I was doing."

"You didn't tell him!"

"Of course not. That's all Greg needs. This is a small town, Lisa. Opinion becomes fact in a matter of days. I told Dad I was doing you a favor."

It was more than a favor. Gillian was the only anchor available in a storm that began the moment Lisa had seen the missing child poster.

And even though she was terrified of the answer, Lisa whispered, "What did you find out?"

ELEVEN

Before Gillian could answer, a man welcomed everyone and directed them to turn to page 180.

"I'll tell you after church," Gillian whispered.

Church consisted of announcements, prayer, singing, another prayer, the Lord's supper—which Lisa had never seen before—more singing, a sermon—*long*—the invitation song and a final prayer. If Lisa had any thoughts of talking after the final prayer, they were dashed when a crowd of people came over to be introduced.

Lisa, however, wasn't the only center of attention. A number of people wanted to know why Perry was sitting on one side of the church and Gillian on the other.

"We're taking a break" was all Gillian said. Grabbing Lisa by the arm, she dragged her down the aisle and to her parents and growled, "Probably a permanent break." Before Lisa could respond, Gillian continued, "Mom, Lisa's coming to the house for dinner, okay? And, I'm going to go ahead and ride home with her."

"We've been wanting to meet you," Gillian's mother said. "I'm so glad—"

Gillian dragged Lisa away before the conversation went any further.

Once they got to Lisa's car, the words poured from Gillian

before she finished securing her seat belt. "This Alex Cooke is some character. Every news story I found claims that his wife disappeared either Tuesday evening or Wednesday morning. Last time she was seen was Tuesday evening. She was playing in the yard with their daughter, Amy. No one knows how Amy got to school the next morning.

"His workday started out routine. Employees say he arrived first, seemed in the usual mood, all business. Then, just after noon he disappeared. Later, he claimed he went to use the restroom. Instead he came in the front door, robbed his own bank, killed a man and, on the way out, he accidentally lost his mask. He's psycho. He looked right at the surveillance camera. He had to know where it was. If ever a man needed prayers, it's that one."

Lisa could only nod. Prayer wasn't her first instinct, but it seemed to help Gillian.

"Then," Gillian continued, "he had the audacity to show up ten minutes later, acting surprised and claiming he'd been stuck in the restroom."

"I think I remember the story," Lisa said. "My sister, Tamara, couldn't stop talking about how amazed she was by how calm, and then how surprised, Alex Cooke appeared when he returned to the scene just minutes later."

"Tamara's the lawyer?" Gillian asked.

"Yes. I listened to her and her boyfriend discuss the case."

"Most of the news stories figured Alex Cooke killed his daughter, too. Some even speculated that he also killed himself. Well, at least they found his wife's body and evidence that he brought her flowers. Hey, do you have the poster?"

Using one hand, Lisa dug the poster out of her purse. Gillian looked at it for a moment and said, "Yeah, I downloaded this one, too. Did your sister, Tamara, think he killed his daughter?"

"She never mentioned it. Being a typical lawyer, she was more interested in where the money and the gun ended up. According to her, having just ten minutes to hide it narrowed the window drastically."

Lisa parked the car in front of Gillian's house, leaving the driveway for her parents. They hurried in, shed their coats and headed upstairs, with Gillian leading the way. Lisa came to a dead stop the moment she stepped inside.

"I know." Gillian, apparently noticing Lisa's perusal, sighed and looked around her room. "It still looks like it belongs to a high school student. When I moved back, I left it alone because I thought it would be temporary, allowing me to save money for my wedding, while Perry worked on getting job security."

"How long is that taking?" Lisa asked.

"So far, six years longer than I expected. And, truth be told, I think I've stopped expecting anything ever to happen."

Lisa looked at the mounds of paper Gillian had printed out the night before. She had them scattered on the floor, on her desk and even across her bed. Luckily, there wasn't much else in the bedroom or Gillian might be in trouble.

Gillian took a folder off the desk. "The information seemed to take off in so many directions, I finally sat down and made folders to help me keep track. I labeled this one BANK ROBBERY. Alex Cooke robbed the bank he managed way back in—"

"How did he get his daughter back? Why isn't he in jail?" Lisa sat on the edge of Gillian's bed, careful not to knock papers to the floor. All of a sudden, she wanted her coat back. The heater working overtime in Gillian's parents' home wasn't strong enough to chase away the kind of chill Lisa was feeling.

"He's not in jail because he escaped before they could arrest him. He got his daughter back because he was extremely lucky. Amy Cooke went to morning kindergarten and then had a playdate scheduled after school. Amy's teacher said it wasn't unusual. The other mom took the two girls to a movie and then out for ice cream. That's how she missed hearing the news. Alex caught up with them just as they were getting home from the ice cream place. He told the other mom that his wife was sick and in a matter of moments he and Amy were out the door."

"How did he escape from police custody?"

Gillian tossed Lisa a printout. It took Lisa just a minute to ascertain that Alex Cooke had simply walked away from a Kansas jail just five minutes after being taking to the interrogation room. "Cooke got lucky again. A fight between two rival gang members, out in the booking room, caused the officer to stick his head out of the interrogation room door. Apparently, a body went flying by, the officer jumped out to block anyone from jumping on the guy. Momentarily, everyone's attention was off Alex and he just walked out of the police station."

"And he just walked away." Lisa put the BANK ROBBERY folder aside and picked up one labeled FAMILY. "That was just, what, eight months ago."

"A few months before Greg landed in Sherman," Gillian admitted.

Lisa opened the folder and took out its contents. The first one was a missing child's poster identical to the one Lisa had swiped. Lisa studied the photo of Alex Cooke. Now that she thought about it, it was also the same one that had been on the television when school started. She remembered sitting in the auto repair shop, waiting for her car—the car Greg Bond had hit—to be fixed, watching the grainy black-and-white television, and thinking that the bank robber, Alex Cooke, had nice-looking eyes.

She'd never considered that the robber looked like Greg. For the first time in almost twenty-four hours, she felt a thread of hope. Maybe she was wrong.

Okay, she was willing to follow Gillian's example. Lisa *prayed* she was wrong.

A car pulled into the front driveway. Doors slammed and laughter sounded. Gillian walked to the window and looked out. "My parents are home. We have at most thirty minutes before lunch is ready. We need to pack this stuff up and take it to your place. I don't want my mom finding any of it."

"What else do you have?" Lisa asked.

Gillian picked up another folder. "I downloaded pictures of Amy and Rachel."

"Rachel?"

"Alex Cooke's wife."

There were five photos of Amy in all. Each one showed a little girl who could easily pass for Amber Bond. Amber was a little taller, a little slimmer, but the smile was the same and so were the eyes. Still, Lisa reasoned, there were lots of fairhaired preschoolers who looked like Amber.

Rachel Cooke was an older version of Amy and definitely an elegant beauty, as was the house she stood in front of.

Yup, bank managers made far more than teachers.

Somehow, it was hard to imagine Greg living in such a house, a house that definitely showed the signs of a skilled landscaper. The house Greg lived in now, a rental, was a little blue Victorian that needed painting. Even the yard in the photo of Alex Cook's home didn't seem like it belonged to the Greg she knew. Greg's front porch—at least the one time Lisa had been there—had a bike tossed haphazardly on it, along with a plastic yellow table with crayon marks on the top. There'd also been chalk drawings on the uneven and cracked sidewalk. Thanks to the onset of winter, the grass had been yellow, brittle, and in some patches, missing.

"They're not the same man—no way," Lisa admitted, almost

giddily. "It's just a case of two little girls who look a lot alike. I guess I got spooked."

"I understand," Gillian said softly, "because when you called last night I couldn't stop thinking about how last year when Greg helped with our spring carnival, he handled the money. I remember being impressed with how accurate his accounting was." Her words got even slower. "Not only did he sort the ones, fives, tens, twenties, but he also turned all the bills so they were facing the same way."

Lisa looked back at the photo of Rachel Cooke. She was holding onto a black, wrought-iron handrail that flanked three steps leading up to a veranda. She had on cream-colored slacks that looked wrinkle-free. They were topped by a matching orange-and-cream top. She had on heels. Her blond hair was swept up in a French knot.

She was beautiful.

And much too lovely to be dead at such a young age.

The two women studied the picture silently. Gillian broke the silence. "I said from the first week I met you that I thought you and Greg were a perfect match. There's just something between you two. I don't know what it is. No way is he Alex Cooke."

"I remember your telling me that he was a perfect match for me right before he smashed into my car."

Gillian sat next to Lisa and hugged her. "Well, he got your attention, didn't he?"

Yes, he'd gotten her attention and kept it. He'd also kept his promise to fix her car. Silently, Lisa read one computer printout after another. The Cookes' entire history, especially the six-month period between the bank robbery back in February and the more recent August discovery of Rachel's body, was available to the world via the click of a mouse.

Suddenly, Lisa stood so fast papers fell off the bed. "He hit my car!"

Gillian looked confused. "Yes."

"Right about the time Greg hit my car, they found Rachel's body. I was watching the television coverage in the waiting room at Vince's brother's car repair place."

"Yes, so what? What are you trying to say?"

"What was the date they found Rachel's body?"

Gillian bent down, rummaged through the folders on the ground, and came up with the one labeled RACHEL COOKE. She quickly thumbed through it and came up with a paper. "Her body was discovered on August 18."

"What day of the week was that?"

Gillian ran to her desk and flipped her calendar. "Wednesday."

Lisa smiled, her whole body relaxing. She almost felt like celebrating. She did feel like celebrating!

"Gillian, that's *the day* Greg hit my car. No way are Alex and Greg the same person. The news is claiming that Alex Cooke took flowers to the farmhouse the morning the body was discovered. According to the news, judging by their condition when the CSI team arrived, the flowers were put there between six and ten in the morning. The teenagers showed up about eleven. Even taking that earliest time, six, there's no way Greg could have left flowers and gotten back to Sherman. I saw him at seven, when I arrived. He was busy working on the school parking lot, that paved-in section, that morning, and later he was busy hitting my car!"

Monday morning Greg dropped Amber off at school, knowing that the snow falling on his windshield spelled trouble. He would be driving three hours to meet Burt halfway, and for the first time in eight months Greg would not be able to get to Amber in ten minutes' time.

He was tempted to take Amber with him.

He was tempted to turn around, stay in Sherman, tell Burt to do all the driving. But Burt was excited and apparently on a roll. He claimed he didn't have a day to devote to travel. For the first time, Burt was talking about closure, solving the mystery, giving Greg back his life. Burt had names, dates and suspicions. It was only three hours to Minden, Nebraska, where Burt wanted to meet.

The windshield wipers pushed at the snow, and gray was the color of the day. The radio played tune after tune of music Greg either didn't know or had forgotten. Sometimes he felt as if his whole life were as much a haze as the gloomy October weather.

Except for Amber.

She was the sunshine that made every step he took worthwhile. She didn't deserve the fugitive life, didn't deserve to have to change her name and hair color. For months, up until Rachel's body had been discovered, he'd blamed himself. He'd done something, maybe while in the foster-care system, maybe while climbing the corporate ladder.

Burt no longer believed there was any chance that Greg was the catalyst, and finally Greg agreed. The target had been Rachel, and Greg was in the way.

Burt said they were ready to take the next step.

Greg wanted the same thing: to find Rachel's killer, *finally*. For Amber.

Minden, Nebraska, was a hardy little town about the size of Sherman. It was a bit more of a tourist trap, thanks to a place called Pioneer Village, but October didn't draw many tourists. Burt had come up with the name of a diner and just before noon, Greg slid into a booth.

Right at noon, Burt walked in, leather bag bulging and a grim look on his face.

He held up a pretend coffee cup at the waitress and sat down. He didn't greet, he didn't hesitate, he jumped right in. "I'm convinced the killer intended for Rachel's body to be found. There are too many clues. One, did you realize the body was found on the six-month anniversary of her abduction?"

"I did."

"The cops noticed the date, too. They didn't think it was a coincidence. They think you wanted to shake things up a little, get some attention."

"If that was the case, why didn't I shake things up a bit earlier? Six months is a long time."

"The Friday before Rachel's body was discovered, the lead detective on the case retired. Rachel's case was already on the back burner. His retirement pretty much took the case completely off the stove: cold. I'm thinking the killer didn't like that much."

Greg could only shake his head. *How would the killer know?* The waitress chose that moment to stop by the table with Burt's coffee. Both men ordered the special of the day, and as soon as the waitress was out of earshot, Burt went on.

"You already knew that the body wasn't discovered sooner because that particular bedroom had always been locked. Something the cops didn't leak was that the lock on the door was fairly new. Obviously put on by the killer when he deposited Rachel's body. Unfortunately, it's a standard—what?"

Greg winced and said, "I'm still not comfortable with thinking of Rachel as a body."

"I'll say what I've been saying all along. You think of her as a body. You get mad! Being melancholy only causes you to drag your feet. We have to find this low-life scum. You know what else he's done? He's put flowers, white daisies, once a month, in that room. Sometimes he purchased them in Yudan. Sometimes he purchased them in Topeka."

"You found all this out?"

"No, the cops found all this out."

Greg sobered. Somehow, for some reason, he hoped Burt would be one step ahead of the cops.

"Look, we're going to get this guy. And, hey, there's always a positive," Burt said. "I now know more about flowers than I ever dreamed possible."

"Such as?"

"Such as there's a daisy for every season—I bet you didn't know that when you picked it for your wedding—and they all have two names: one you can pronounce and one you can't."

"I didn't pick them for our wedding. Rachel did. Daisies were her favorite, from the time she worked at the florist. Hey, what—"

"Already been there. I found the woman who owned the shop when Rachel worked there. Since she'd already done it once for the police, it only took her a minute to write down the names of everyone who worked for her during Rachel's time. There were only a few. Rachel and Diego were both student workers, then there was another full-time florist and then two drivers. The owner's not under suspicion. The other florist is deceased. Of the two drivers, one has moved to Florida—retired. He's on oxygen. Pretty much a cripple. The other driver still lives in Lawrence. He drives a school bus. He and his wife are raising their three grandkids. It's not him."

"What about Diego?" Greg wouldn't have picked the man. But, the connection was there. "He's on our list of three. Is there any other connection?"

Burt took a moment to answer. He bit into eggs that Greg knew were cold. It didn't seem to bother him.

"You know, I'm still working on three names, but they're not the same three. Diego is not a suspect. He's doing his second tour in Iraq. He's got a solid alibi. I'm not too crazy about spending any more time investigating Robert Thomas, either. He has a job in Washington at the Smithsonian. I've talked to his coworkers, friends, the minister at his church, even the waitress at his favorite restaurant. They all say the same thing. He works twelve-hour days by choice. He has to be forced to take vacations. And his vacations do not correspond with Rachel's murder or the robbery."

Greg tried to feel relieved. According to Burt, two people were off the list of suspects, but three remained. Greg should be ecstatic. Maybe there was a light at the end of the tunnel. Maybe…

"You could have told me all this on the phone. Why did you make me meet you?"

"Two reasons. First, I truly think this part is important or I wouldn't have brought you here, I want to see your face when I show you some pictures about the last two from my original five." Burt pushed his empty plate aside and laid three pictures down. One he moved forward. "This is Dan Anderson. I like him as a suspect because he's an accountant—the numbers connection. He's your height, a little heavier, but, hey, he could wear a girdle or something. Does he look familiar?"

Greg picked up the picture. The man looked like a typical accountant: short hair, white button-down shirt, black shoes. "No, I don't remember him from the wedding or the reunion. I've never seen him."

"He didn't attend either, at least by invitation. None of Rachel's friends think so, either," Burt said. "Dan's married, one child. He golfs, like you, plays racquetball, like you, and he spends more time away from his family than with them."

"All like I *used to* do."

"He travels a lot, even to Wellington. He's currently having an affair. His wife doesn't know. I'm wondering if maybe he approached Rachel, flirted a little and was turned down." Burt paused, leaned back into the booth, and crossed his arms.

Greg took the hint and looked at the photo again. Nothing. "Did they know each other?"

"Possibly. He did the books pro bono for the theater Rachel worked at."

"It had been years—"

"Maybe he harbored a grudge." Burt pushed over the last two pictures. "Then, there's Christopher Engstrom. He's a bit older than the others. He's a janitor at Lawrence High. He's never had a student or teacher lodge a complaint. His flaw, according to a teacher I spoke with, is he misses work a lot. I haven't been able to get his file, yet, but I'll be looking at workdays missed and how they compare to the bank robbery and Rachel's discovery. He worked at the school while Rachel attended."

"I've never seen him, either," Greg said.

"Well, he's your height, although nothing else is similar. He's forty-two but looks and acts more like sixty-two. Neighbors say he doesn't leave the house much, except to go to work. I guess there was never a father, and his mother died a few years ago, so now he lives alone." Burt opened his briefcase and took out another picture. Greg did recognize this one.

"Tony Buckman—the jock."

Burt nodded. "Christopher, Tony and Dan are pretty good leads. Did you know that Rachel broke up with Tony during their senior year of high school?"

"Yeah, she mentioned that."

"I guess he was devastated. Missed school, moped. I guess the coach and his parents really had to talk some sense into him. He was ready to quit both school and sports. I got this piece of information from two of Rachel's girlfriends."

"So we have three suspects. Good. I'm still not convinced I

needed to drive all the way to Minden to look at pictures you could have faxed me."

"As far as Christopher Engstrom goes, at one time his mother cleaned houses as a second job. For three years, while Rachel was in sixth through eighth grade, Mrs. Engstrom was their family's domestic help. Still, he's not my personal favorite." Burt looked uncomfortable as he reached into his coat pocket. "Dan Anderson is. And not just because of his current affair. I also tracked down his last mistress. She claims he broke the windows in her car and made a nuisance of himself with phone calls."

He laid the final photo on the table, facing up. "There's this last picture. This is really the one I needed to give you in person."

Greg took the photo. It had at one time been a five-by-seven but someone had trimmed it, probably to fit in a wallet. Slightly wrinkled as if it had been taken out and put back a few times, at first, it looked like a typical relationship photo. Woman in man's arms, fairly intimate embrace, woman smiling, man kissing.

Dan Anderson, the cheater, and Rachel.

TWELVE

Greg's hands shook. His throat closed. He took a sip of coffee and coughed it up. He started to stand, but Burt motioned him down.

"I'm almost done. A photo alone is not proof of an affair."

Greg opened his mouth, but his throat was still closed. Words were impossible, and judging by the look on Burt's face, there was more.

"One of Rachel's friends confirmed the affair. I guess it didn't last long. It was—"

Greg's throat finally opened. "Why'd you ask if I knew him? Why didn't you say this from the start?"

"Believe me, I went back and forth on whether to meet. But, in the end, I needed to see your reaction. It's going to be important. If I've sniffed out the affair, it's only a matter of time before the police do. I'm pretty amazed they haven't already." Burt sobered. "Of course, they might know. They might be keeping the information under wraps until they catch you." Burt shook his head. "The truly ironic turn to finding out about the affair is that you're sitting there feeling betrayed, and I'm sitting here knowing the cops will confirm your guilt."

"This just—" Before Greg could continue, his cell phone rang. It was his babysitter's next door neighbor. Seemed Lydia

Griffin had stepped out onto her front porch twenty minutes ago and slipped on some ice. The neighbor saw the whole thing.

Greg hung up. Great, just great. His babysitter was in the emergency room at Sherman Hospital and Sherman Elementary dismissed, what, two minutes ago. He held up a hand, hushing Burt, and made a quick phone call to Amber's school.

It wasn't lost on him that just minutes after finding out that his wife had betrayed him, he was already turning to the only person in Sherman he really trusted—Lisa Jacoby.

"Everything all right?" Burt asked.

"Yes and no," Greg answered. "I've got to head home. Amber's teacher has agreed to watch Amber until I get there. But Amber's fine. The babysitter's a bit battered. My life is so out of control, I…" he stopped. "I *do* know where to turn. I've got a three-hour drive in snow coming up. Did you know that the last time the weatherman talked blizzard in October was more than a decade ago. And it's coming now—right when I least need to deal with it. Thank God I have God to talk to. He's going to get an earful."

Burt put a twenty on the table, more than enough to cover breakfast and a decent tip for the waitress. He shrugged into his coat and walked with Greg to the truck. "I hate to give you even more, but as long as you're going to be talking with God, you might as well talk to him about one more issue."

Greg's hand stilled on the door handle. It crossed his mind to tell Burt to just stop, not say anything. That it was more than one man could handle.

"Go ahead," Greg ordered instead.

The wind had already burnished Burt's cheeks to a ruddy red. One hand clutched his briefcase—the other hand, he was holding onto a piece of paper, regular notebook paper, already growing damp from the snow. Great, just great, something else for Greg to look at, something else to shout Your Life *Is* a Mess.

"I told you," Burt began, "early on to keep a calendar. Where you are every day, at what time, and who can vouch for you. Here are some dates I really want you to look at."

"Why?"

"It goes back to the daisies. The cops have been busy showing your picture to florists near the Yudan area. So far, two clerks have identified you as someone who purchased daisies in the last few months."

Monday, at just after three, Principal Mott came to the school entrance where Lisa and the other teachers stood huddled with their students. No one had expected snow like this. It was mad.

As Principal Mott closed in, Lisa felt like her students must whenever someone in authority marched toward them. Her first thought was, *I've done something wrong.*

She was right. While Principal Mott watched the remaining students, Lisa went inside and took a call from Greg. He sounded a bit frantic. "Mrs. Griffin fell and broke her leg. I'm out of town at a meeting. Even if I leave now, it will take me three hours to get home."

"Is Amber already signed up for after care? You want me to walk her there?" It was on the tip of Lisa's tongue to suggest that next time Greg should tell Principal Mott his dilemma, but then even as she heard him protesting, she remembered the first day of school, Greg's words: "I know you've been given the students' records but I wanted to make sure you were clear about Amber's… I'm a bit of an overprotective dad. Besides me, the babysitter, Mrs. Griffin, is the only one allowed to pick up Amber. Amber doesn't go to after-school care and she doesn't go home with other children."

Amber doesn't go to after-school care.

"I'll watch her until you get here."

"Thank you. I'm running to my car now."

"Greg, you don't need to run. I've got her. We'll have a fine time. She can play in my room, and then I'll take her to get something to eat if you're running late."

"I will not run late."

Principal Mott raised an eyebrow but didn't question beyond, "Is everything all right?" Amber, on the other hand, was ecstatic. She was staying with her beloved teacher.

"I'm having an adventure," she announced to the other children.

Later in the classroom, her adventure started with erasing the boards, halfway; straightening the desks, her definition of straight; and sorting students' papers into their cubbies. That last was everyone's favorite duty and when Lisa suggested it, Amber rewarded her with a hug. Finally, the list of chores Lisa could provide ended and Amber sat down at her desk to draw.

Staring at Amber, Lisa felt a sudden longing. There were a few teachers on staff who had their own children at Sherman Elementary. It was actually fun. Amber had chattered, but not so much that Lisa couldn't work.

Amber's chatter went something like this: *Mikey stole my eraser today, but I didn't tell you because he gave it back.* Followed by, *My daddy plays on his computer as much as you play on yours.* And Lisa's personal favorite. *Tonight's Wednesday. We always eat at Sonic on Wednesday nights before we go to church.*

The little girl's chatter stirred a longing in her.

Someday, Lisa wanted children: children who'd stay after school with her, help in the classroom, chatter, give hugs.

Of course, melancholy longings did not get the work done and report card conferences started tomorrow after school. If Lisa didn't finish tonight, she'd have to come in early.

In college, they didn't spend enough time teaching education majors how to fill in report cards. Lisa had completed twenty so far. They were the easy ones. The ones where she got to type: *Doing well*, or *Improving*, or *Top of the class*. They were already printed out and waiting on the corner of her desk. Five still needed her attention. Four were for students who desperately needed some positive reinforcement. Lisa had already written drafts of what she'd be telling the parents: *It's early in the school year*, or *Improvement might be just around the corner*, or *Need to work harder*.

The last blank report card belonged to Amber Bond. For some reason, it seemed to be the hardest for her to write. Maybe since Amber was in the room. Or maybe because every time Lisa thought about Amber, she thought about Greg, about her suspicions, and about the way Greg made her feel.

Lisa studied the little girl in front of her. Amber didn't act like anything was wrong.

Ask her about her mother; how she died. The thought came unbidden, and Lisa rejected it almost immediately. It would be taking unfair advantage of Greg's asking her to watch Amber. She also didn't want to inadvertently scare Amber, especially since she didn't know how the child's mother had died or what memories she would be unleashing.

She had a vested interest in both Amber and Greg. They, in a short time, had become a part of her life.

Lisa had looked up the distance between Sherman, Nebraska, and Yudan, Kansas. It was five hours. Yes, Greg had appeared distracted the day of the wreck, but he hadn't looked exhausted. Besides, what about Amber? If he'd taken her with him, she'd have been exhausted. And, if he hadn't taken her with him, it meant he'd left Amber all alone.

Nope, not something Greg would have done.

End of story, again. Greg Bond and Alex Cooke were not the same person.

Lisa typed in a password that brought up her students' files, specifically their last year's grades. She was only interested in one.

The copy of Amber's kindergarten report card showed an average student who had trouble concentrating. No surprise. It was always difficult to adjust to entering school during the last month. It made Lisa wonder why Greg hadn't just kept her home.

There was nothing in Amber's file to spark suspicion.

"Amber, I'm leaving the classroom for just a minute. I need to get something from the office. Don't leave."

Amber was busy drawing and just nodded.

A moment later, Lisa was back in the classroom with Amber's paper file in hand. Everything in it was a copy, no surprise. Still, a magnifying glass and an overactive imagination showed a couple of areas where someone might have forged information. On Amber's birth certificate, certain letters looked a little crooked. Amber's mother's name was Melissa. Then, on Amber's immunization record, the print looked faded in spots and bold in others.

"If you look deep enough," Lisa muttered, "you'll find something to worry about."

"What?"

Lisa looked up. She'd gotten so used to talking to herself, in the classroom that she'd forgotten that Amber was there.

"Nothing," Lisa joked.

Amber didn't smile. She looked serious for a change. She was looking out the window.

"Amber, Honey, your dad will be here any minute."

Amber nodded and went back to her drawing.

The lights blinked once, twice, and then again. They'd been doing this all day while the snow fell. Lisa glanced at her computer. Time to get to work. She hadn't typed a word in almost an hour. She'd been too busy thinking about Amber and her dad and about a file that had all the "right" information but somehow felt wrong.

She had files at home, too. She and Gillian had gone through pages of information about Alexander Cooke.

Wait a minute.

On her desk, she had Amber Bond's history. At home, she had Alexander Cooke's history.

What about Greg Bond—his history?

She took the computer out of sleep mode and clicked on a browser. Then, she typed in *Gregory Bond*.

Lisa wound up with a dozen hits. None of them had a connection to Sherman, Nebraska. None of them was about a construction worker with a small daughter.

The first Gregory Bond was listed on a passenger list of a downed plane. Another Greg Bond, this one with more than half the listings, was a professor at a New England university. He'd attended many conferences and had earned plenty of awards. Another Gregory Bond was listed in a wedding announcement. Then there was a store owner. Last, she found a Gregory Bond who was a missionary in Africa.

Her Gregory Bond, hovering parent, handsome construction worker and mystery man, didn't have an Internet presence. No surprise there. Lisa Jacoby didn't have much of an online presence herself. The only place her name appeared was on a list naming last year's college graduates at the university she'd attended.

Lisa checked on Amber, still drawing and starting to look a little tired. Next Lisa glanced at the clock, almost six, and then looked out the window. The sun was quickly fading. Plus, there was something about being alone in a school building after dark that made Lisa think of horror movies, loneliness and vulnerability. Suddenly, she felt spooked. Surely the principal was still here or a janitor or two. Lisa thought about standing up, going outside and making sure everything was all right, but doing so seemed like a sign of weakness, and she didn't want to frighten Amber. Besides, this was *her* classroom.

She glanced out the window again. The last few rays cast jagged shadows on the blanket of graying snow. How many times this week had Lisa stared out the windows at home, looking at the dark lines and shivering. Not from the cold but from an unsettling feeling that somebody was out there, somebody was watching her. And now the feeling had followed her to school.

Maybe it was because, most definitely, except for school events, this was the latest Lisa had ever lingered.

Lisa clicked on an icon and brought up Amber's report card. Maybe she should do one more, then leave. Amber truly was doing well in school, except for her penchant for drawing when she should be doing work. The kid was quite an artist. Lisa could always tell what Amber was drawing, be it a person, an animal or a place. She hadn't mastered proportion, but she nailed colors and details.

Amber had drawn a picture of Lisa that was so cute, Lisa framed it and hung it in the classroom. The best thing about the picture was that it made Lisa taller and thinner. The cute thing about the picture was how Amber detailed Lisa's shoes, the orange ones. Then, she had Lisa in her favorite blue dress, not that she wore her orange shoes with it! And, last she'd put Lisa's bright red whistle—the only bright red one any teacher at Sherman Elementary boasted—around her neck. Amber didn't miss a thing.

"Daddy?" Amber whispered.

Who, if Lisa wasn't mistaken, was standing by the tree near the street. Lisa stood, walked to the window and tried to get a closer look. Amber came and stood next to her. What was Greg doing, just standing there in his tight red-and-black-plaid jacket, jeans and black gloves. Even he looked spooky now.

He raised a hand and waved.

Then, he walked away.

"Daddy?" Amber whispered.

Strange.

"I'm sure he'll be right in," Lisa soothed. The words sounded false even to her. What was going on? Why was Greg standing outside? If it weren't for Amber, Lisa might have headed outside and chased Greg down, but Amber's silence stilled her. Instead of returning to her desk, Lisa got a piece of paper and some crayons of her own and then settled at the desk next to Amber. It was enough. Amber gave a half-hearted smile and returned to her drawing.

It was stranger still, ten minutes later, when Greg walked into the classroom.

"I cannot thank you enough. It just kept snowing and the drive took me longer than I thought. I'm so sorry." He rubbed his hands together. They were red from the cold.

"I'm ready!" Amber announced. "Daddy, what took you so long to walk inside?"

"Huh?" Greg paused. He'd already taken Amber's coat from the hook. He picked up her backpack.

"We saw you outside," Lisa explained as she stood and walked toward her desk. It was past time to get home. "Remember? You waved."

"I…" He shook his head, acting a bit shell-shocked, and stuttered, "I… You saw me outside! When?"

"About ten minutes ago," Lisa said as she took her purse out of her desk's bottom drawer. "Amber's right, you even waved. Are you all right?"

Greg rubbed the back of his neck. "I'm fine."

"Yeah, Daddy, I waved and you waved back."

Greg didn't look fine; he looked pensive. Then he seemed to shake it off as he said to Amber, "Honey, it must have been somebody who looked like me."

He took the drawing tablet she offered and put it inside her backpack.

Lisa sat, hard, clutching her purse and watching Greg Bond. *He wasn't the man outside?*

Could the man outside have truly been someone else? Amber seemed willing to believe her daddy. Lisa wasn't so sure. Same coat with a hood, both wearing jeans. The chill Lisa felt might be from the cold and might be from suspicion. Could this man be Alexander Cooke? Could he have kidnapped Amber?

The lights faded, flickered a bit, and then finally brightened. Amber scurried to her dad. He put a hand on her shoulder. Every move, every look, every word and even the wavering smile showed a devoted father.

Lisa quickly started to gather papers and put them into her bag. She could finish the last of the report cards tomorrow during her break. She needed to get home, think and maybe even follow Gillian's advice: pray.

All day the lights had been testy. The kids had been testy, too.

"It's Wednesday night. We're going for hamburgers now," Amber said. "Want to come with us?"

The students often invited her places without parental prodding or knowledge. She'd been invited to countless birthday parties, at least three weddings, a baptism and even to Saturday night roller skating.

Greg answered for her, "I'm sure Miss Jacoby has plans."

Nope, no plans. It probably took more than three months in a new town to find a circle of friends.

"I do appreciate the invitation, but I have a few more report cards to fill in," Lisa said. "I think I'll go ahead and fill them in at home tonight. The lights keep flickering here. It's distracting. Then I find myself either playing on the computer or looking out the window. It's just an eerie night. I can't shake the feeling that somebody is out there. If it wasn't you, then who?"

Greg was already guiding Amber toward the classroom door. He abruptly stopped, drew Amber close, and tersely asked, "Where was the guy who looked like me?"

"Outside, by the big cottonwood tree."

"How long ago again?"

"I'd say about ten minutes before you showed up. And it wasn't you?"

"No," he said slowly. "It wasn't me."

Greg and Amber waited while Lisa turned out the lights and locked the room. Greg positioned himself in the middle, as if he needed to keep a hand on both of them. He held Amber's hand tightly. He was so close to Lisa that when she slipped, all it took was a hand to her elbow to steady her. The contact was momentary. Yup, at the moment, he was the Greg Bond she knew so well. The one more interested in checking out the street than in checking out her.

A moment later, he was checking out her car, which refused to start. "I'm not a car person," he finally said. "I'm sure it's just the cold or something. Maybe we should call Vince." He took out his cell phone, punched in the number and, after a moment, he left a message.

Putting his phone back in his pocket, he said, "I'll give you a lift home—"

"No," Amber whined. "Come eat with us. You'll have fun."

Greg looked like fun was the last thing on his mind. He also looked frozen.

"Where are your gloves?" Lisa asked.

"Daddy never wears gloves," Amber said. She sealed Lisa's fate by adding, "Daddy, I'm hungry. It's been forever."

"Sonic is on the way to your place," Greg said. "And treating you to a meal's the least I can do as thanks for watching Amber." He reached over and plucked her book bag from her arm. His hands were red from the cold.

"Really," Lisa protested. "You don't have to."

"We had fun," Amber announced. "I'd rather stay with Miss Jacoby than Mrs. Griffin." Then, as if suddenly feeling guilty, she said. "Is Mrs. Griffin okay?"

"We'll call her later," Greg promised. "After we eat."

They trudged to Greg's truck.

He'd had no intention of inviting Lisa along for supper. Never mind how bad a mood he was in, how devastated, he couldn't walk away from her car and leave her there. He tried telling himself that he owed her, that having her with him gave him one more witness to his whereabouts, but it felt wrong, hollow. The closer she got to him, the closer she got to danger.

Unfortunately, it looked like she was already too close for comfort. Rachel had once told him that she waved at somebody she'd thought was him.

They'd laughed it off.

He'd never laugh off woman's intuition again.

He hoped Lisa didn't think of this as anything more than a father thanking his child's teacher. He worried that he had invited out an innocent bystander who might have seen something she shouldn't.

Lisa wasn't a female to woo; she was a witness to interrogate.

Amber, however, was beside herself with happiness. Her beloved teacher was accompanying them for a meal. Once they settled into the truck, Amber's "on" button activated and a continual one-sided monologue resulted. According to Amber, right now everything was fun. School was fun. Winter was fun. Going to church was fun. And now having Miss Jacoby join them for supper was fun.

Greg just drove, grateful that the snow was letting up, and all the while watching in front of him, behind him and on both sides.

He didn't doubt Lisa's word. She'd seen something.

His cell phone rang, ending Amber's conversation, and momentarily interrupting Greg's worries about whatever, *whoever,* it was Lisa thought she had seen.

Burt didn't waste any time on salutation.

"Greg, I told you there were two reasons I wanted to meet in person."

Yeah, Greg remembered the first reason. His best friend wanted to watch Greg's face when he found out that his wife had been unfaithful.

"Your phone rang before I had a chance to tell you the second."

"I can hardly wait," Greg mumbled. "Shoot."

"I had you meet me in Minden because both Dan Anderson and Chris Engstrom live in Lawrence now. They gotta know I'm asking questions. If either of them is the killer, he's got to be watching me. I'd hate to lead him to you."

THIRTEEN

It had been a while since Lisa had eaten at Sonic. And, she'd never taken advantage of in-car dining during the winter months.

Three people in the front seat of a truck had more disadvantages than advantages. Mainly space. Luckily, Greg believed in using his heater.

Lisa took off her mittens, stretched her fingers and tried to think of something to say. She'd never considered herself shy, but sitting here with Greg and Amber didn't feel, well, school-teacher-ish. It felt more friendly.

When you have at one time half suspected a man of kidnapping his own daughter, the idea of friendship can become awkward.

Amber certainly didn't act kidnapped, or distressed or sad. She sat in the middle, every once in a while eagerly grinning at Lisa, and then she divided her time between talking and drawing. Greg looked on, ever the proud parent.

Nope, definitely not Alex Cooke.

Luckily, the food didn't take long to arrive. Amber handed her drawing tablet to her father and set her drink on the open glove box door. Following the example of an eat-in-the-car pro, Lisa followed suit. Then they used the dashboard for their burgers.

Some of Amber's ketchup dripped on Lisa's shoe. Amber

giggled. Greg looked bothered, but he'd looked bothered ever since he'd hung up his cell phone. Whatever was bothering him wasn't the ketchup.

The meal would have been silent save for Amber. Without her drawing tablet, and with a captive audience, she rambled on about the schoolday, about the snow and about her favorite TV shows.

About the time the food disappeared, Amber perked up even more.

"Look, Daddy. Tiffany's family just parked."

"It's the Wednesday evening rush," Greg explained to Lisa. "Sonic's near the church, everyone's in a hurry and no one wants to cook."

Since the front of Greg's truck truly only fit three, Amber soon negotiated a change of venue. She joined Tiffany's family.

The moment Amber exited, Lisa realized that everyone in Tiffany's family was staring at Greg's truck, at who was inside. Greg and Sherman's new first-grade teacher, that's who.

Greg didn't seem to notice the stares or consider what Tiffany's family might be thinking. He pulled the drawing tablet from the floor, set it between them and finally looked at Lisa.

"I was wondering what made you think it was me you saw outside the classroom window."

She'd almost forgotten. "The man was your size and height, and he was wearing the same kind of clothes."

"Winter clothes, you mean?"

"I mean he had the same kind of coat, same hat, everything," Lisa agreed.

"Have you ever seen him before?"

"Maybe," Lisa admitted. "At our last softball game, there was a man in the park who caught my attention. He gave me the willies. I'm not sure why." She paused, looking at Greg and not liking what she saw. "Ever since that night, I find myself looking out my apartment window. Every once in a while it seems like there's a shadow or two that moves like a human."

She half expected Greg to scoff or maybe reach over and pat her shoulder. He didn't. Instead, he went back to watching the Taylors' van, the top of his daughter's head for a moment before asking, "The guy you saw at the park. Was he dressed like me?"

"No."

After a moment, Greg reached over and took her hand.

It was all he needed to hear. There was someone out there who looked a little like him and that someone was watching Amber and now Amber's teacher.

Holding Lisa Jacoby's hand wasn't going to keep her safe; changing Amy's name to Amber was no longer keeping her safe.

Looked like Burt decided to watch his back about a week and a half too late. It was time to get out of Sherman. There'd be no church service tonight. Funny, church had so *not* been a part of his life before the robbery and Rachel's disappearance. Now, it was a cherished piece of his life for him to forfeit, for Amber to forfeit. Goodbye church, goodbye friends, goodbye life. As soon as whoever was following them might be asleep—please let the man feel safe enough to sleep—the Bonds were gone, both literally and figuratively.

Now, Alex had to figure out someone else to be.

After checking his watch, he let go of Lisa's hand and gathered up both his trash and Amber's. Lisa quickly collected hers. She didn't mention the handholding, but her cheeks were a bit red.

He shouldn't have taken her hand. Yes, it had felt good to touch a woman, comfort a woman, but not now, and certainly not when he knew the woman's heart was his for the taking.

"I'll throw this stuff away and get Amber. It might take me

a minute. She's not going to be happy." He knew he sounded curt, and judging by the expression on Lisa's face, she wasn't too impressed with his attitude.

Good.

He didn't blame her.

He certainly wasn't good company. Three hours ago, he'd discovered that his wife had cheated on him. Thirty minutes ago, he'd discovered that her killer probably had been sharing the same Sherman zip code as his for at least three weeks.

It had been three weeks since their last softball game. Lisa had seen something, felt something—it was enough to convince him. He could only hope that the killer didn't realize that Greg was on to him.

Snow stuck to his boots. The cold swirled around his hands, and he put them in his pockets. His cheeks felt the bite more than any other part of his body. Good. He needed to be awake tonight. He intended to drive.

Where? He wasn't sure. He'd have to trust God to navigate.

"Hey, Greg." Tiffany's mother rolled her window down an inch. "Amber can drive to church with us if that's okay."

"I appreciate the offer, but we might be skipping church tonight—"

"Dad! I—"

"Don't get to argue," Greg finished.

"We heard about Lydia," Tiffany's mom said. "The prayer chain is already going strong. They called her son, who lives all the way in Denver. He'll be here sometime tonight. You did hear the terrible news, didn't you?"

"Yes, I had to get Miss Jacoby to watch Amber after Mrs. Griffin fell."

"I'm not talking about the fall," Tiffany's mom said. "I'm talking about what caused the fall."

"Ice on her porch." Greg opened the backdoor and held his hand out to Amber. "She's that age."

"Hmmm, I don't think age mattered much this time. According to her next-door neighbor, the police have already been by asking questions. Seems somebody poured water on Lydia's porch. It was virtually a mini-skating rink she stepped on."

Amber's hand clutched his.

"They think it was kids?" he managed to ask.

"No, they think it was an adult male. They found footprints in the snow. The sheriff and his men are still at her house."

Thursday morning six children were missing from Lisa's classroom. Five mothers called in; all blamed the snow for their children's absence. One father didn't call. Lisa wondered if whatever it was that was bothering Greg had something to do with Amber's absence and his lack of a phone call. No one seemed worried.

"It's because he lost his sitter," Gillian supposed after they'd gotten their lunches and sat at the teachers' table in the lunchroom.

"No, he'd bring her to school and take off work early to come pick her up," Lisa argued. "Besides, Mrs. Griffin is already out of the hospital and at home. Amber'd be more of a help than a hindrance."

"Hmmm," said Gillian. "Not so sure about that, and I'm thinking Mrs. Griffin's son might not think so."

Gillian had a point.

"Okay, you win. Maybe Amber's just got a cold like everyone else. Speaking of everyone else," Lisa queried, "what's up with Perry?"

"Nothing's up with Perry."

"You saw him last night at church, right?"

Gillian scowled. "He was there. I was there. He sat by himself in the back. I sat with my parents. Hardly anyone was there. Snow has that effect on people."

"Were you hoping he'd talk to you?"

"Hmmm," Gillian made a face. "I'm not sure. I noticed him when he arrived, but felt absolutely no urge to go back and sit with him, which is unusual. Even my dad noticed."

"What does your dad think about somebody pouring water on Mrs. Griffin's porch?"

"Dad doesn't think a kid did it. Dad says Lydia Griffin was wild when she was young and has a few enemies."

"Enemies? Lydia Griffin?" Lisa couldn't even fathom that. "Wow, did your dad say what kind of wild?"

"No, I think he regretted saying it within my earshot."

The bell rang and chairs scraped as the last of the lunchtime stragglers headed for the tray turn-in and then the gym. No one got to go outside today. The wind chill alone acted as a deterrent.

Gillian gathered up her trash and stood, tapping her foot. "I can't believe you let me drive you to school this morning and didn't say a word. And now I've waited all through lunch for you to tell me, but I guess I'm going to have ask."

"Ask about what?"

"You had dinner with Greg and Amber last night."

Yes, she had. And all night she'd thought about it. Staring out her apartment window, for the first time the shadows hadn't seemed human. She'd carpooled to work this morning with Gillian and spent the entire ride filled with anticipation, looking forward to Greg dropping off Amber, maybe saying something.

Anything.

Instead, Amber didn't come to school.

Finally, Gillian stopped tapping her foot. "Don't think I'm not going to ask more questions later. Right now, I'll cut you some slack. I have papers to grade."

Gillian walked out the door, and Lisa looked at her food. Most of it remained on her plate. She thought about picking up her fork, taking one more bite, and just trying to get on with her day, but before she could act, she noticed Jake Ramsey, the town sheriff and fellow softball player, standing in the cafeteria doorway.

The world of elementary school adults was primarily female. When an over-six-foot-tall man walked in, people noticed.

He sat across from Lisa. She put her fork down.

"Jake, something wrong?"

"I don't know, but maybe. You talk to Greg lately?"

"I watched Amber after school yesterday. We went to Sonic to eat dinner afterward."

He held my hand.

"About what time did you leave Sonic?"

"It was probably around six-thirty, maybe six forty-five. He goes to church on Wednesday night. It starts at seven."

"He didn't go to church last night," Jake said. "I know because I did. He wasn't there."

"Well, Amber invited me to go with them. Maybe after they dropped me off at home he decided it was too late. The roads were starting to get bad."

"Greg's old truck puts most to shame. That wouldn't make him miss church."

Lisa pushed her tray to the side. "Why are you asking these questions? Is something wrong?"

"I'm sure you heard about the ice on Lydia Griffin's porch. I wanted to ask Greg a few questions. See if he had any ideas. He called in sick to work yesterday, and today he called and told the foreman he'd be out for more than a week, but didn't say why."

"Hmmm," Lisa said. "He didn't act sick yesterday, but something was bothering him. He was distracted. Amber and I thought we saw him outside a good ten minutes before he walked through my classroom door. We even waved. Then, when he did arrive, he said it wasn't him. I believe him. It still spooked me."

It was on the tip of Lisa's tongue to say more, but another bell rang, this one alerting both students and teachers that lunch and recess were over.

Jake stood. "I've been to Greg's house. The truck's gone. The screen door was open, but the main door was locked. Something doesn't feel right. I walked around a bit, peeked in the windows. I wasn't the first person making tracks in the snow outside his windows. By the time I realized that, I'd made a mess. Boy, am I kicking myself because I'm wondering if the same adult male who poured water on Lydia Griffin's porch also did something to Greg. I've called his cell at least five times. You wouldn't happen to have another number for him?"

"No, just his cell and work. I don't think he has a landline. At least, he didn't give the school another number."

Jake frowned. "You need to get going. I've seen what kids can do if the teacher runs late. If you've got any ideas, I'd appreciate hearing them. Are you going to be in your classroom after three?"

"Yes, and I'd really like for us to meet."

No, not really. Meeting with the sheriff about Greg Bond was the last thing Lisa wanted to do. Something was wrong— so wrong the sheriff had showed up at school. It was time for Lisa to pull out the missing child poster and run it by someone besides Gillian.

Lisa didn't know how she'd make it through the afternoon.

The sounds of children—laughing, pushing, screaming— echoed through the hallway. She could only hope their noise would erase the accusations assailing her.

She should have called the missing child number weeks ago, when she first found the poster. Not only had she put Amber in danger, but she was jeopardizing her own career.

And Gillian's.

Walking into her classroom, Lisa blinked against the bright lights that contrasted with the gloom outdoors. It was a gray day. Even the kids felt it. They were somber as they wriggled in their seats. Teaching math probably wasn't the best idea. The students would be zombies.

"Let's do free reading for a while. You can even sit under your desks."

The "Yeahs!" were unanimous. In moments, the mood of the room brightened a bit.

Lisa walked around, helping the youngsters choose books, then identifying words and even turning some books around so they weren't upside down.

When she got to Amber's empty desk, she paused. Because Amber had stayed late the night before, it was clean. No papers stuck out the sides, no pencils were on the floor. There wasn't even glue residue on top.

It looked wrong, just plain wrong.

Lisa opened the top.

Amber's stuff was crammed inside, including some of the drawings Amber had done yesterday after school. Lisa picked them up. The top one was of outside the classroom window. Amber had colored the snow gray.

There was the parking lot with two cars. Amber made them both blue, and snow covered them. There was the street with no cars. Amber remembered the fire hydrant at the corner. From the classroom window, three trees could be seen.

The creepy man from yesterday was there, too, next to the most distant tree. Red-and-black-checkered coat with a hood.

Blue jeans. Amber hadn't seen his shoes; they were buried in gray snow. Amber had drawn the man as he was waving one black gloved hand. The other hand was behind his back.

The second picture was of Lisa at her desk.

The last picture was of Greg and Amber in front of their house. They were doing what families were supposed to do in the wintertime—making a snowman.

Maybe all of Jake's worries were for nothing. Greg had gone out of town yesterday; maybe today he'd done the same, only this time taking Amber with him.

By the time three rolled around, Lisa was ready to scream. The students, as if sensing their teacher's mood, had been pensive all afternoon. They'd yawned during art, spilled beans all over the floor during math time and acted as if they'd never seen a vocabulary word before during spelling time. Outside, the snow didn't let up. It came down continuously, living up to the word *blizzard*.

At three, Lisa and the other teachers stood inside the entrance and waited for all their charges to be picked up. Outside, the sky turned even darker.

Gillian kept raising her eyebrows. Clearly, the news that Jake Ramsey—Sheriff Jake Ramsey—had stopped by to see Lisa, had spread throughout the school. No doubt the lunch ladies had heard enough to know it wasn't a social call.

"My room?" mouthed Gillian.

Lisa shook her head and mouthed back, "No, mine."

A few minutes later, with the door firmly closed, and after Lisa shared every word Jake had uttered, both Lisa and Gillian studied the missing child poster for the umpteenth time.

"I still don't think Greg Bond and Alex Cooke are the same man," Gillian said.

"Greg's gone. I know it. And Jake thinks there's a connection between what happened to Mrs. Griffin and Greg's leaving."

"That's really a stretch," Gillian argued.

"What kind of man packs up his daughter in the middle of the night and disappears?" Lisa muttered. "That's not normal. It's not healthy."

"It probably happens more than we know," Gillian said. "You and I—we just grew up lucky. We never struggled."

"You think Greg and Amber are struggling?"

"They live in a rental. Greg mentioned being in the foster system. He's also a construction worker, at the bottom of the Konrad Construction food chain. It's winter. Work tapers off. He knows it. It's either head to where there's work or go on unemployment. I have the idea Greg's proud."

"You think I would have sensed something yesterday. He took me to dinner. He—"

"Called you from out of town and had just lost his babysitter."

"You know what's really bothering me?" Lisa said, as she sat down at her desk and put her head in her hands. "What's really bothering me is that I'm half in love with him and yet you have more faith in him than I do."

"Ah," said Gillian. "But I've been raised on faith. Maybe we should say a little prayer right now."

Lisa's head was already bowed.

Valentine, Nebraska, was not a hopping place in the winter. Of course, hopping in two feet of snow was never a good idea anyway.

Bending down, Greg took Amber by the hand, hoisted her up to her feet and made sure she was far enough away from the street. Back in Sherman, she would have giggled and tried to pull him down into the snow. Way back, when they lived in Wellington, maybe she'd have grabbed a handful of snow and instigated a snowball fight. With her mother. Because Greg would have been at work instead of with them.

He brushed Amber off and said, "We're going to be all right." He almost added, *I promise* but he couldn't manage the words.

They'd been in Valentine one day and the only word he could think of to describe his daughter was *subdued*.

Someone had followed Burt from Lawrence to Sherman. Someone had been watching Greg and Amber for weeks.

Someone...

"Daddy, you're squeezing too tight." Amber pulled her hand from his grasp and promptly fell down again.

"Daddy, where are we going?"

"Back to the motel?" It was a mere block from the Pizza Hut, where they'd just eaten.

"Do I have to go to bed?"

"No, you can play or watch television."

"Will you play with me?"

He took her hand again, this time making sure not to squeeze too hard. "I'd love to play with you."

Two hours later, he'd turned out every light but the one in the bathroom. He left that door open so he could see enough to work. Amber slept on the second double bed. She clutched at her pillow.

He had to come up with another name—Amanda or something. This time changing their identities would probably be more difficult. She'd started to like being Amber. Of course, she missed being Amy.

First things first. Greg headed to the bathroom and dialed Burt. All last night and all day today Greg had been trying to reach Burt. The man did not answer his cell.

It was Burt's only flaw. If he were busy or just didn't want to talk, he didn't bother answering.

Greg was pretty much guilty of the same thing. Right now he had nine missed calls, all of them from Sherman. Looking up most of the numbers had been easy. Five calls came from Jake Ramsey, the sheriff. Four calls came from the sheriff's office. Not good news. One number he couldn't identify.

Because Amber was sleeping, Greg couldn't even voice his frustration. This morning he'd rearranged the room. Sitting down at the small table he positioned next to the bathroom, he turned on his laptop.

He almost wished he and Burt corresponded by e-mail, but Burt said no—no paper trail. Too many times in court, e-mails were the damning evidence.

What to do first? Try to come up with new identities for them, or see if he could find out what was going on in Sherman. He decided to keep track of things in Sherman, curiosity as to the number of calls from the local sheriff getting to him.

Sometimes it took hours to find a bone; sometimes it took minutes. Tonight Greg found what he was looking for in a matter of seconds. He found it on the *Sherman Tribune*'s Web site. There was a story about Lydia Griffin's accident and whether or not it really *was* an accident. Already twenty-three posts offered opinions. Wait, maybe that was twenty-two posts. One wasn't really interested in Lydia Griffin. No, that post was for Greg. It was the ninth comment down.

You're not taking care of her.

Greg's gut said, "This is aimed at me." But common sense replied, "Stop reading threats into everything!"

Since nothing had made sense since the day of the bank robbery, he wasn't surprised by the fifth comment down.

If you don't take care of her, I will.

She's not Rachel, but she deserves more.

FOURTEEN

Jake Ramsey hadn't shown up after school on Thursday, missing his meeting with Lisa. There'd been a three-car pile-up, with one fatality, on Main Street. Instead, Lisa had gone out to eat with Gillian.

They'd rehashed all the Alex Cooke information, segued into analyzing Greg and Perry and then talked shop. Lisa didn't tell Gillian about Greg holding her hand. Maybe it was because Gillian would read too much into the gesture. Maybe it was because, after thinking about it *all day,* Lisa realized that Greg might have attempted to comfort her with his touch, but he hadn't attempted to comfort her with his words.

He hadn't said, "In Nebraska, during the winter, there are always shadows."

He hadn't said, "We all look alike in our bulky, heavy coats, knit hats, heavy boots and gloves."

He hadn't said that she shouldn't worry.

So she worried.

"In twenty years," Gillian said, after they'd finished their meal, paid their tab and headed toward the door, "we'll laugh at this. I mean, come on, if a bank robber, murderer, kidnapper, came to hide in Sherman, he wouldn't stay long." They stepped out into an all-white world. Snow covered everything.

It came down in bulk. It graced the trees, the car tops, and hid the sidewalk.

"I mean, think about it. There's absolutely nothing to do here," Gillian said seriously.

Lisa shuddered. "Stop thinking about it," Gillian urged, not even waiting for Lisa to say anything. "We'll tell Jake. We've harbored these suspicions long enough."

"I know," Lisa agreed. "He'll laugh it off."

"And eventually," Gillian added, "Greg will laugh it off, too."

Friday morning, Lisa wasn't so sure. Today ten children were absent, all the teachers were grousing that this should have been a snow day and, at noon, Mrs. Griffin called.

"Lisa," she said, "have you heard anything from Greg? I just got a note from him thanking me for watching Amber this last year and with a week's pay."

It took Lisa a moment to digest Mrs. Griffin's words—what they really implied. Finally, she managed, "Amber's not in school. She was absent yesterday, too. The note didn't say you were fired or anything, did it?"

"No, but the sheriff came by this morning asking questions. He seems to think that someone poured that water on my porch anticipating that Greg would be the one to walk on it. It would have been Amber, first, and then maybe Greg, but I thought I heard something and stepped out to see."

"What did you hear?"

"A noise on my front porch. I'm old, that doesn't mean I'm deaf."

"But you didn't see anything?"

"No, the cops have asked me that question five different ways. This morning Jake was asking me about Greg. Then, when I got his note, I knew it was something serious. What's going on?"

"I don't know. Something's on his mind, but I'm not the one he'd tell."

"No, but you're the one Amber'd tell. That little girl talks about you all the time. Has she said anything?"

Funny, Mrs. Griffin didn't sound scared or even nosey, for that matter. She sounded concerned.

"Not a thing," Lisa murmured. "Not a thing."

"Well, I think Greg's in trouble," Mrs. Griffin muttered right before hanging up.

Lisa hung up, too, her fingers trembling as fear slammed into her gut. Either Greg was *in* trouble or he *was* trouble, and no matter which one it turned out to be, she was involved.

How was she going to make it through the afternoon?

Taking out Jake's card, she thought about dialing the number. She could go to the principal, take the afternoon off and head for the police station.

That's what she should do if she really thought Greg *was* trouble.

Problem was, she was more inclined to think he was *in* trouble and that her insinuations would only get him *in* deeper.

She put the card away. She'd know tonight when she told Sheriff Jake Ramsey her suspicions.

The thought of what she had to do trailed Lisa from reading groups, to a spelling test, to a restroom break. As if feeding off her mood, the weather worsened. By the time three rolled around, Lisa was more than ready to head home. She wanted to call Jake: tell him to come over now, no delay. Maybe he'd tell her they'd found Greg, this was all a mistake, and he was glad to know someone was worried about him. She wanted to turn on the television, find out that hundreds of innocent drivers were caught on the interstate and that snowplows were trying to dig them out. Surely Greg would be one of them. She wanted to curl up in bed and dream that Amber had a cold, and that Greg had kept his daughter home, and oh what a surprise that everyone was looking for them.

Of course, none of those scenarios explained the note and severance the pay Mrs. Griffin had received.

"You want to spend the night at my house?" Gillian asked as they walked to the car. "It might be safer."

"If you're convinced that Greg is really Greg and not Alex, why are you worried about my safety?"

"I'm more worried about your sanity," Gillian joked.

"I'll be fine. I'll watch the news, call my mother and veg out."

"You call me if the sheriff or someone important stops by."

Lisa knew the *someone important* was Greg, but he wouldn't stop by. He no longer called Sherman home.

And, feeling a bit heartsick, Lisa realized just how much she'd miss him, *whether he deserved it or not.*

Jake Ramsey thought so, too. He knocked at Lisa's door just after seven. The minister, Miles Pynchon, was with him. Lisa turned down her television, grabbed sodas from the refrigerator and sat at her kitchen table. Miles sat across from her.

"Greg's gone. His clothes are gone, his laptop's gone and some of Amber's clothes and toys are gone." Jake paced.

Lisa's apartment had never looked so small.

"I've been all over town. John Konrad, his boss, is surprised. Mrs. Griffin is surprised—"

"I know. She called me," Lisa said. "She's insisting that something sinister is going on."

Jake stroked his mustache. "That sounds like old Lydia. She used to hang about with my granddad, back when he was sheriff. He called her 'colorful.' The town called her lots of other things. Most not so good."

"Any chance she has something to do with this?" Lisa asked.

Both Miles and Jake shook their head. "She was a wild child who took time to settle," Jake said. "In the last fifty years, she's been married, been widowed, raised a son and gained everyone's respect."

"Maybe she made an enemy who took a while to find her?" Lisa suggested.

"She wasn't that wild," Jake said. "Besides, between my granddad and me, we've known her over fifty years. If something was amiss besides that patch of ice, we'd know it."

"Lisa, can you think of anything that might help us," Miles encouraged. "If Greg's in trouble. He'll need friends."

It was on the tip of Lisa's tongue to protest, *Why come to me? He's just the father of one of my students.* But, as private as Greg was, really, she was the logical choice.

"There *is* something," Lisa began. "But it's too outrageous to be true."

Jake stopped pacing and leaned against a wall and waited. Lisa now had a full view of her living room, of her television. "What?" Jake demanded when she didn't continue.

It took Lisa a moment to process what she was seeing: a crime scene, something fuzzy, an ambulance. Then she jumped up, only to stand frozen in place until, finally, the victim's face came into focus. And Lisa was sure. She knew the man.

With only three strides, she reached the corner of the room. She turned up the volume and sank to her knees. But the only thing on the TV now was footage of the police cordoning off a crime scene.

The news commentator droned on about the Alex Cooke case.

Jake sank to his knees next to her. He turned up the volume, listened and demanded, "What?"

The phone rang, loud, jarring. Only the preacher seemed to notice. Lisa knew the caller had to be Gillian.

No doubt, she was watching the news, too.

"I met him in front of Greg's house last month," Lisa said, pointing to the man's face that was once more on the television screen. "He claimed to be an insurance salesman."

Was it really only last month? Yes. October and Open House at school. Amber had the chicken pox. She and Gillian had taken over soup.

"His name is Burt Kelley."

One thing for sure: Jake Ramsey processed information quickly. Lisa showed him the wanted poster and the pages she'd copied from Gillian. He sat still for all of three minutes, flipping through the information and muttering, but not looking all that surprised.

Then he sprang into action. She and the preacher were treated to the type of one-sided conversation that inspired more questions than answers.

They sat mesmerized while he first called his office. They heard him ask for the name of Alex Cooke's wife, they heard what she thought was Greg's address and orders for someone to head over there, and they heard Jake order someone to come over and stay with Lisa.

That was the moment Miles raised one eyebrow and looked at Lisa as if to say, *What have we gotten ourselves into?*

She wanted to answer, *More than we can chew,* but the sheriff was still talking. Lisa heard enough to figure out that Burt Kelley was still alive, barely. She heard enough to figure out he was a bounty hunter instead of an insurance salesman.

Had Burt Kelley been blackmailing Greg?

They'd certainly seemed more like old friends.

When Jake stopped shooting off questions and issuing orders to whoever was on the other end of the phone, he started issuing orders to Lisa. Both Lisa and the minister were ordered not to talk to anyone about what they'd just discussed. She was not to leave the apartment until Jake returned. The minister agreed to stay with her until the deputy—who was apparently now assigned to guard Lisa—arrived.

"You wanna tell me why you kept this information to yourself?" Jake asked.

"I kept waiting for something besides his daughter's looks to convince me that he was anything other than what he appeared to be—a nice guy."

Jake's expression didn't change. He was no longer teammate, no longer a friend. He was all cop. "Gillian's in on this, too? Is there any chance she and Greg had a relationship before you came along?"

"Besides being his daughter's teacher, neither of us have a relationship with Greg." Lisa paused. "Well, there's church. Gillian and I took him a casserole once. You know about softball."

"I know about softball. I've seen you and Greg together," Jake said, "which is why I think you're the target.

"I'm sending over one of my deputies. Answer all her questions. I'm going to send someone to talk to the Magees, too. Just in case Gillian's in trouble. Do you have someone you can stay with? Like the Magees? I don't want you alone."

Lisa barely had the strength to nod. "I'm sure the Magees will let me stay with them."

"Good." And then Jake was out the door with his cell phone pressed against his ear.

He was not a happy man.

Good, because Lisa wasn't a happy woman.

Just as Greg hadn't told her to stop worrying about the shadows, to stop thinking she was seeing someone who looked like him, Jake hadn't reassured her that Greg Bond and Alex Cooke could not possibly be the same person.

This was bad, bad, bad.

And Lisa was in so much trouble—she was basically under house arrest. And she was a target!

Lisa picked up the phone to call Gillian, but before she could dial, the doorbell sounded and Gillian was there, bursting into the room and shouting, "Did you see the news?"

Silently, Lisa pointed to the minister.

Gillian raised an eyebrow. "Reverend Pynchon. What are you doing here?"

"The Bible calls it ministering to the flock. Today, I'm calling it damage control."

"Huh?"

"Jake asked Miles to come here in case I needed someone to talk to," Lisa explained.

"Wonder why he didn't ask me?" Gillian mused.

"I think he was planning to visit you next, but got more than he expected here," Lisa said. "Jake asked me if you and Greg had any kind of relationship. I told him no."

"Maybe if Perry hadn't been around," Gillian sobered. "Hey, this is serious. What does Jake think? Are Greg and Alex the same person? Are we in trouble?"

Lisa simply nodded. "I think we're in trouble."

Lisa, more so than Gillian. She'd found the poster of Amy Cooke and noted the resemblance. All along, she'd been more concerned than Gillian.

Gillian had waffled about calling the authorities because of faith—faith in Greg Bond.

Lisa had waffled, because of her heart.

"And Gillian," Lisa said, "you need to get home. Jake is sending someone over to talk to you."

The minister held up his hand and looked around the room. "Lisa, do you have a Bible?"

"No."

"Good thing I brought mine. I was thinking maybe this was the time for scriptures, but maybe we need prayer." The reverend seemed a bit disoriented. No doubt this was not a typical evening spent ministering to his flock.

Miles folded his hands together. Lisa watched as the minister bowed his head and was silent for a minute. Then the man breathed in, out. When he raised his head, he looked a lot calmer, more self-assured. He'd obviously regrouped.

Prayer did that?

"Ladies," he said.

Gillian bowed her head. Miles waited until Lisa also bowed hers. He didn't say a long prayer; he didn't judge; he only asked for God's wisdom and God's watchfulness. After he uttered *Amen,* he turned to Gillian and said, "I think Lisa's correct. You need to head home. Plus, you'd two shouldn't to be together talking about the case until after you've talked with the police separately."

He continued, "If it comes to court, you wouldn't want a good lawyer claiming you collaborated."

Collaborated? Court? As if she and Gillian didn't talk about everything already! Lisa looked over at Gillian, whose eyes were glued to the television. Burt Kelley's face was back on the screen. Lisa had turned down the volume, but hadn't turned it off.

Gillian looked at Lisa. Lisa stared back helplessly.

Greg Bond and Alex Cooke were the same man.

The morning news did more than report on the weather. Burt Kelley's face and yet another crime scene linked to Alex Cooke spurred Greg into action. It only took him twenty minutes of sorting through the hotel's dumpster to find a wrinkled receipt with a credit card number. An hour after that, he'd parked his truck in a grocery store parking lot and they'd walked to a car rental place just minutes before they'd closed. He'd gotten lucky. The young kid running the place wanted to get off work—it being Friday night and all—about as much as Greg wanted to get out of town.

He'd have a lot to answer for when this was all over. He'd lied, stolen and put loved ones in danger—all to protect Amber.

Well, at least he was doing that, and now, thanks to some crazy man who posted insane messages on news blogs, Greg needed to protect Lisa.

He was pretty much at a loss. Whom should he call? Plenty of people wanted to talk to him, but none of them would really listen. He couldn't call the hospital in Lawrence, where Burt had been taken. They wouldn't give information out except to family members. Burt didn't have any family. He couldn't call Lisa. She'd urge him to turn himself in. She was way too naïve to understand the position she was in.

He finally decided to call Jake Ramsey.

Jake picked up on the second ring.

"Jake," Greg said. "Good, I can't explain, but I need you to listen to me. Lisa's in trouble—"

"Where are you?"

Greg had hoped to have a few more days, hours, before the Greg Bond cover was blown. Jake's no-nonsense tone closed the lid on any chance of that.

"I can't tell you, but I guess you're not asking because you're just curious."

"We've already run your prints, so, no, Alex, I'm not curious," Jake said.

Alex. It had been almost a year since anyone besides Burt had called him that.

"I'm making this short." Greg gripped the steering wheel. Once again, no one was on his side, no one was willing to believe him, and this time he didn't even have Burt to turn to.

Almost immediately, the thought came to him: *You have God to turn to.*

It was enough. "Look, Jake, I read a blog on the *Sherman Tribune*'s Web site. Somebody referenced Rachel. I think whoever killed my wife might be watching Lisa."

"I read that blog, too, Alex. I'm pretty amazed that you had the audacity to post such a thing. Turn yourself in, Alex. It's just a matter of time before the authorities—"

"Me? You're accusing me of posting that comment! What do you think—I'm a split personality or something?" Greg was spitting mad. If just one sane person would open his eyes to the truth, so many could be saved.

Then Greg almost choked as Jake's words sank in. "What makes you think I posted the comment?"

"FBI's already here, Alex. They tend to act quickly when tracking a man who has killed twice."

Okay, there was a reason for the hardened voice, the no-mercy tone. In Greg's nightmares, it was always his wife's face that haunted him. He saw the guard's face, too. The man had been a long-time colleague.

Jake was still talking. "They traced the source to a network at the Sherman Library. The one you and Amber like so much. The librarian remembers seeing you Thursday night."

On Thursday night Greg was already in Valentine. He already had a motel room, and he was already working on stealing their next identity.

The truth didn't sound like much of an alibi.

But that was beside the point. If the librarian had "seen" Greg on Thursday night, Greg had something else to worry about. "The post on the news site came from Sherman? From the public library? You sure?"

"I'm sure. Where are you, Alex? Tell me where you are. I'll—"

"You need to keep Lisa safe," Greg said. "And I'm not the one who's threatening her. I need you to look into both Dan Anderson and Christopher Engstrom. They—"

"Both have alibis. We're not stupid. The Feds already know your connection to Burt. They know that he was working for you. Let me escort you in. Make sure you're safe."

Safe? Greg didn't ever expect to feel safe again. But if he could keep Amber safe, that would be enough.

No, wait a minute, it wasn't enough. There was somebody else who deserved to be safe.

The killer was still in Sherman.

And the cops were looking for the wrong guy.

Greg had to head back.

FIFTEEN

"Who were you talking to, Daddy?" Amber said groggily.

Greg wished Amber had stayed asleep. Hearing her voice only reminded him that whoever was stalking them didn't care who he hurt.

It was a stupid, stupid move. Was there really a best-case scenario? One that had him driving through Sherman unde-tected, warning Lisa *and* getting her to actually believe him, and then him managing to drive out of town again?

No matter which way he looked at it, the worst-case scenario seemed the more likely.

"I was talking to Jake Ramsey, the sheriff. The man who pitches for the softball team."

"I know who he is, Daddy."

Greg knew who he was, too, which is why it made no sense, this inner drive that had him heading back to Sherman because of Lisa.

She wasn't his responsibility.

This was God's fault.

The God who said, *Love one another*. The God who said *Take care of my sheep*.

Well, this shepherd had a disposable cell phone and knew Lisa's number by heart.

She answered on the second ring.

"Lisa, this is Greg. I know what I'm about to say sounds crazy, but—"

He heard muffled voices in the background, and then someone took the phone from Lisa. "This is Officer Gayle MaGuire. Mr. Cooke, you need to turn yourself in."

He hung up the phone.

Same song; different singer.

Yet the background noise nearly caused Greg to lose control of the car. He could hear Lisa protesting *his innocence.*

And Greg was humbled. From the beginning, he'd been struck by Lisa's innocence. Still, the old Greg, Alex, wouldn't have thought twice about taking care of himself and leaving her alone to face the enemy. The new Alex, Greg, not only thought twice, but also lost sleep and was putting Amber in danger to protect Lisa.

He could only pray that God would direct the eyes of the law to look elsewhere. Maybe they'd be looking for his Greg Bond persona—black hair and blue eyes.

What Greg had now was pretty much a light brown. The box called it some silly name, and it made him look a bit too much like Alex Cooke now, a bit too much like his wanted posters. Amber's hair was the same color. Greg wondered if it were a sin to hope the police saw the wrong Alex and took aim.

Probably.

"Daddy, why did you call Miss Jacoby?"

"There was something I needed to tell her."

Luckily, six-year-olds didn't always need elaboration. Amber changed the subject. "Where are we going?"

"Back to Sherman."

Amber sat up. "We're going home."

"No," Greg said quickly. Sherman was no longer home.

Really, it had never been. He'd stayed there too long, though. "We just need to stop, see your teacher for a minute and then— I think, *I hope*—we're going to Lawrence."

"What's in Lawrence?"

The blood trail led to Lawrence.

"A friend."

Two friends, actually. Burt Kelley was in a hospital in Lawrence. Greg shuddered to think that while Greg and Amber had been fleeing Sherman, the killer had been in Lawrence.

And in Lawrence was the only other person who might still believe in Greg—Shelly Moser, the head librarian where the first post to a news blog had been made. Greg intended to show up on her doorstep. He wanted to know if she knew what Burt had been planning to do Friday night. He wanted to know everything she knew.

First, he needed to convince Lisa to head to Tucson, stay with her sisters, hire a bodyguard, something.

As he pulled onto Lisa's street, he started to pray. It wouldn't be easy.

Oh, wow.

The squad car parked in front of her apartment was the first deterrent. The shadows from at least one other person came second. If Greg wasn't mistaken, Reverend Pynchon owned the truck parked across the street. Great, just great. Greg had expected to deal with cops. He'd half expected to have to deal with Gillian. But his minister? What was *he* doing at Lisa's? Was she hurt?

Greg drove slowly. Good. He could see Lisa's shadow in front of the window. She was moving just fine, so maybe the minister was praying.

Praying for Lisa's safety, Greg's arrest?

Greg's safety?

If that were the case, right now Reverend Pynchon's prayers were partly answered. Lisa was safe, for the moment. Greg was safe, for the moment. And, yes, it looked as if Greg were certainly doing all he could to ensure his own arrest.

Coming back to Sherman was a stupid move.

Glancing in the backseat, he checked to see if Amber were still sleeping. She was. He pulled down the road and parked between two cars. Then he turned off everything. Climbing over the seat, he took the DVD player from Amber's hand. He shut it off and grabbed two blankets from the very back. They'd do. It was after eleven. The minister surely wouldn't stay much longer. Greg wasn't sure about the cop. If he remembered correctly, Officer Gayle McGuire had two small children and was quite happy handling traffic and other light duty.

She was also the only female officer Sherman boasted. Chances were, if Jake wanted someone to stay with Lisa, who better than a female?

Wait! If Jake had assigned an officer to stay with Lisa, then Greg didn't need to worry. Jake was taking the situation seriously.

Greg shook his head.

No one took it as seriously as he did.

He'd kept Amber safe all this time, as disturbing as the thought was. It looked like the time had come to keep Lisa safe, too.

Not because he had to, but because he wanted to.

By the time the police officer followed Lisa to Gillian's house, there was no doubt. Greg Bond and Alex Cooke were, indeed, the same person. Prints had been taken from his house and matched. On the off chance that Alex—would she ever really think of Greg as Alex—was still in the area, the local police were out in full force.

Not that they expected to get much done in the middle of a Nebraska blizzard.

Lisa figured this out thanks to eavesdropping. In the last hour, in between myriad questions, the officer had fielded at least ten phone calls.

By the time they left for Gillian's, Lisa felt like a criminal.

It was only a ten-minute drive, but it gave Lisa way too much time to think. And the more thinking she did, the more convinced she was that Greg/Alex was innocent. Somehow, no matter what the evidence, she knew that he was innocent.

Tamara always said the truth was in the small details, not the large one. Well, then it was time to think small.

Taking out her cell phone, she ignored Jake's order and called her sister. It was about time to take advantage of having a lawyer in the family.

Unfortunately, right now, Tamara was a lawyer who didn't answer her phone at…

Lisa checked her watch. It was midnight in Nebraska, that made it eleven in Arizona.

She'd get no help from Tamara tonight. It really gave Lisa pause because if the police could make her feel like a criminal, *and she wasn't,* what might they do to Greg?

No wonder he never talked about his wife or his past.

They had his picture on a surveillance camera, robbing his own bank.

The man she knew wasn't that stupid.

The female officer stopped in front of the Magees' house, got out of the car and with her flashlight motioned for Lisa to wait while she checked around the house. After a moment, she escorted Lisa from the car to the house. Gillian opened the front door before Lisa had a chance to knock.

"Anything suspicious happen tonight?" the officer asked.

"No," Gillian's dad said. "I've got neighbors on both sides keeping a lookout just in case."

That news didn't seem to reassure the police officer. "You call us if anything seems out of place." She looked at Lisa. "Got it?"

"Got it," Lisa said.

Gillian's father returned to the living room, where he took his wife's hand and went back to watching the news.

"I think it's too soon for news coverage," Lisa murmured.

"I do, too," Gillian said as she led Lisa up the stairs, "But to leave the television off during a crisis just isn't in their nature. They keep expecting a bulletin."

The guestroom was open. Lisa put her bag on the bed and walked to the window. It almost felt dangerous to pull aside the curtain and look at the darkness outside. The police cruiser was still parked in front of the Magees' house. Most of the houses were dark. For the most part, Sherman, Nebraska, was unaware that they'd harbored a murderer close to a year.

"I can't believe Greg is really Alex," Gillian said sorrowfully from the doorway. "He seemed like such a nice guy."

"He didn't do it," Lisa said. "They're acting like he's a split personality or something, but it makes no sense."

"What makes you think so?" Gillian sat on the bed. "I mean, for the last month I've been the one insisting that he couldn't be Alex Cooke, and now that we know I was wrong, that he *is* Alex Cooke, for some reason you're now his champion."

"That officer asked me every question but who I voted for in the last election. By the time she finished, I felt like confessing. It really made me think about Greg. What kind of man he was… is. Every time I was with him, he was focused on Amber. He didn't want her out of his sight. Now that we know he's Alex Cooke, it's all falling into place. All those times we saw him watching the road, not letting anyone but Mrs. Griffin pick up

Amber, acting like he would leave on a moment's notice, he was taking care of Amber. He wasn't looking for the police. He was looking for whoever had killed his wife. He was worried about somebody showing up and hurting Amber."

"You're not a mind reader, and that's a stretch."

"It is," Lisa agreed. "But—"

The phone rang, shrilly, in the still of a night too dark for comfort. They could hear Gillian's dad answer, then they heard the sounds of his steps coming their way. "It's Perry," he said, handing Gillian the phone.

Gillian grimaced and held the phone to her ear. "What?"

Lisa expected Gillian to leave the room. Maybe her dad expected the same thing because he stayed dead center in the doorway. It guaranteed an audience to yet one more one-sided conversation. It didn't matter. After a moment, Gillian took a breath and got started, pacing the room as she talked.

"When was the last time you saw him?… Yes, I told the police everything… Why are you asking me that?… Just because he was friends with Vince Frenci doesn't mean… Okay, it does look bad… I'm not going to tell you you were right… I don't believe that at all… Why? Because it makes no sense. If the Feds were in town over the last few weeks, closing in, they'd have done something to warn us. At the very least, they'd have known when he fled town and followed… Oh, really, Perry, I don't think you're the only one they could trust… I'm hanging up. I'm hanging up."

Gillian rolled her eyes and clicked off the phone. "That man. He says he's not surprised. He said a Fed approached him last week, asking all kinds of questions about Greg and you."

"Greg and me," Lisa said slowly. It would be so much easier to champion him if the "Greg and me" part of the equation hadn't felt, for so long, like such a schoolgirl crush.

"Yeah, Greg and you. But don't worry. Perry's losing it. He's called here every day for the last week. He seems to think if I stop playing softball, stop hanging around with you, quit my job and maybe even change churches, that all will go back to normal—his version of normal."

"It's going to be a while before we see normal again," Gillian's dad said. "You girls need to get some sleep. Tomorrow's going to be a long, long day."

Gillian didn't look like she wanted to leave, but she shrugged and obeyed. After a moment, Lisa was alone. She went back to the window. The police cruiser was gone. The glow from a few streetlights revealed a fairly empty neighborhood. Since this wasn't her part of town, she didn't know if the cars on the street all belonged there.

Feeling more alone than she had in months, Lisa headed for the bed and, fully dressed, crawled in between the sheets. In the morning, she needed to call her mom and sisters. When all this started, the day she found the poster, she should have gone to big sister Tamara instead of best friend Gillian. What was the use of having a lawyer in the family if you couldn't go to her to hear: *You've just tossed your career down the drain. You've just jeopardized a young girl's life.*

If Amber was in danger, Lisa didn't deserve to be a teacher. She wasn't an expert on human nature. But from the first time she met Greg Bond, she was impressed with how he cared for his daughter.

Tomorrow, no doubt, she'd be called to the police station. Who knows what Monday would bring? Losing her job, most likely. At some point, she'd pack up and head back to Tucson, tail between her legs and with a broken heart.

Maybe somewhere in Sherman, Greg Bond was holed up, thinking some of the same thoughts, and…

… and if she knew Greg Bond at all, she knew he'd be praying.

Well, it couldn't hurt.

Tucked under the sheets, in the Magees' guestroom, Lisa said a prayer, all by herself and without prompting. After saying *Amen,* she closed her eyes. She didn't expect sleep, but as if hearing the prayer, and knowing what Lisa needed, she did manage six whole hours of sleep before Sheriff Jake Ramsey and two other men showed up at the Magees' door.

They escorted her back to her apartment.

"What are you looking for?"

"Has Alex Cooke ever been in your apartment?" Jake asked.

"No, Greg's never been up here. He's brought me home from school twice, but I never invited him up."

"Do you mind if we look around?"

She looked at the man, standing there in his white, tucked-in shirt and black pants. No doubt he was looking for some sort of evidence to link her to Alex Cooke. To prove that Alex Cooke a killer.

"Do whatever you want. You don't need a subpoena. I have nothing to hide."

The half smile he gave in return reminded her that she needed to call Tamara.

From her apartment, they went to the school. Mrs. Mott, the principal was waiting. The look she gave Lisa was all business: business—and displeasure.

The three men made her classroom seem small. They walked down the aisle and studied the art on the wall, but only for a moment. What they were most interested in was the man she'd seen from her classroom window. They had her look out, indicating by radio where she'd seen Greg's look-alike. They next went through Amber's desk. They opened every book and spread out Amber's drawings on the floor.

That Amber had drawn the man outside piqued their interest. They handled that picture with gloves and stored it in a giant baggy. They handled each one of Amber's drawings carefully, spreading all of them out on the reading table in back. First, they had Lisa identify when Amber made the drawing and who the drawing was of. They wanted to know the whys, too. They were most impressed with how many of the drawings were of Lisa.

Lisa was back to feeling guilty. The Feds figured she was more than a teacher to the girl, and she could see why. Mrs. Griffin's statements and those of the other softball players didn't diminish that impression.

After a few hours in the classroom, with Lisa re-creating the evening she'd watched Amber, they finally took her to the police station and put her in an interrogation room. Jake, at least, brought her a sandwich.

"If you're hiding anything," he said gently, "you really need to share it."

"I'm being as honest as I can be. The only thing I did wrong was not call that missing child number. And believe me, I wish I had. I'll admit that was a colossal mistake. One I'll probably never forgive myself for. It's just that I couldn't believe Greg and Alex Cooke were the same person."

"I thought I was past being surprised, too," Jake said as he left the room.

Just when Lisa thought she'd scream if they didn't tell her something, talk to her, another police officer entered the room. This one carried a clipboard. He asked her the obvious: name, age, address. He was halfway through a second page when someone knocked at the door. The female deputy from last night poked her head in.

"Her lawyer's here."

"I don't need a lawyer," Lisa insisted.

"You need a lawyer," came a voice both commanding and familiar.

"Tamara!"

Tamara was not the warm fuzzy member of the Jacoby family. That was Lisa's job, and Lisa had never needed Tamara more.

"Do you have grounds for keeping her here?" Tamara marched into the room, and although Lisa knew she had a good inch on Tamara, suddenly Lisa knew that size was relative.

It was the first time Lisa had seen Tamara work a room. The man with the clipboard put his pencil down and said, "She's not under arrest. We're just asking some rudimentary questions."

"How long have these questions been going on? The Magees say you escorted Lisa from their home at eight this morning. It's almost seven. I'm thinking mental abuse, harassment..."

Jake stepped into the room. "And I'm thinking your 'client' withheld information in a homicide case."

"My client had enough reasonable doubt to withhold judgment. Setting an example you'd be well advised to follow. Lisa, are you ready to go?"

Lisa stood. Her legs felt wobbly, but they were in better shape than her thoughts. Tamara started to take Lisa by the arm, but Lisa shrugged her away.

"Oh, baby sister's getting tough," Tamara whispered. "Good."

The police station was about a third full. Perry, of all people, sat in a chair opposite the female officer who'd been Lisa's companion last night.

He looked scared.

"I've been with Gillian for the last hour," Tamara said. "Perry's worried about what all this will do to his political career. Seems he's been talking to someone he thought was an undercover police officer who had questions about Greg Bond.

Perry gave the man the babysitter's name and address, your name and address and they still don't know what else."

Lisa started to say that Perry deserved to look scared, but then she really looked at him.

Was that remorse she saw?

As they were about to leave the station, one of the two officers from this morning beckoned her over. Tamara nodded and said, "Keep it brief."

On a scarred wooden table, the pictures from Amber's desk were spread out, as well as a few pictures Lisa hadn't seen before.

"This one," the Fed said, holding up a drawing, "was taken from the home this morning."

It was a drawing of Greg and Amber and a snowman. Amber was on one side of the snowman; Greg was on the other.

The Fed placed the drawing next to the one Amber had made of the man they'd seen outside the school. The man who Greg claimed wasn't him.

"They're the same," the Fed said. "Red-and-black-checkered coat, black hat. They're the same height."

It finally clicked.

"There *is* a difference," Lisa said. She pointed to the one from the schoolyard. "Look, Amber drew gloves on this man. Her father never wears gloves. He said that when he was a foster child he got used to not wearing gloves."

"That doesn't mean he never wears gloves," Jake said.

"Have you ever seen him with gloves?" Lisa asked. Mental pictures went through her mind. Greg coming into the classroom, rubbing his hands together. Him reaching over, taking her bag from her as they walked to his truck. His fingers red from the cold. Him not seeming to mind.

"I've never seen him in gloves," Jake admitted.

Everyone looked at the pictures again.

SIXTEEN

Greg had been back in Sherman more than twenty-four hours and still hadn't accomplished what he'd set out to do.

When he'd fled Wellington with Amber, he hadn't had time to think. He'd merely reacted.

He tried to picture Lisa, what she was doing, and what she might say when he finally told her who he was and why he'd been pretending to be something he wasn't.

He wondered if she'd believe him, *in him*.

Amber sure hadn't believed in him at first. No wonder. He hadn't been a hands-on father. Truthfully, Greg couldn't remember how Amber had reacted when they'd fled Wellington, other than wanting her mommy.

What he could remember was white-hot fear. The kind that penetrated every pore, until anxiety became a second skin. The only reason he hadn't totally fallen apart from the combination of fear and devastation was Amber. Every time he wanted to give up, give in to what the world around him expected, there she was—sitting in the backseat of the first car he'd stolen, crying.

Okay, he did remember one of Amber's reaction—tears.

This time, she was comfortable with Daddy, comfortable enough to let him know in no uncertain terms that she wanted to go home, she hated being stuck in the van, she was cold, she was bored, she had too many complaints for him to keep count.

He didn't blame her.

He wanted to go home, too, and now that he was back in Sherman, he realized that while he could claim it wasn't home, it sure felt like home, more so than Wellington had.

Those feelings convinced him that he had to get to Lisa, *soon,* convince her that because of him, because he'd allowed himself the illusion that he *could* have a home, she was in danger.

He didn't dare drive by her house too many times. The neighbors were already on the lookout for anything unusual, and although the van said, *carpool mom,* it also said, *I'm new in town. You've never seen me before. So look twice.*

Yesterday, Saturday, he'd taken more chances than he was comfortable with, and he'd never made it within shouting distance of Lisa. He and Amber watched from afar, as Jake escorted Lisa first to her apartment, then to the school and finally to the police station. When the evening shadows darkened and his daughter couldn't watch her favorite movie even one more time on the pint-sized DVD player, they'd driven to Ransome, the next town over, and spent the night.

Greg checked in as a single and made sure that no one saw Amber leave the van and head into the motel.

Today, to his daughter's ire, they were back in the van and cruising Lisa's street. Luckily, the snow had let up and for once the roads were decent. Her street was fairly deserted. There was only one car he couldn't identify, and it was parked right in front of Lisa's house.

Hopefully, it was an undercover officer, maybe even a Fed. Every once in a while he saw movement in Lisa's window— two people. That made his job more difficult, but it did signal that she was safe.

It sure was a pricey car for an undercover operation. Plus, it was fire-engine red. Not one he'd pick if he wanted to keep a low profile.

Greg checked his watch. He needed to get this show on the road. It was just ten. Some people were sleeping in. Others were reading the paper and drinking coffee. Most, in this Sherman neighborhood, were at church.

Jake was probably at church.

Gillian was probably at church.

Greg wished he were at church.

Of the people who mattered to Greg most, and he could count them on the fingers of one hand, only Lisa, Vince Frenci and Burt didn't know the sanctuary God offered.

How odd that the people he knew most at risk in their earthly home were the two most at risk with their Heavenly home, too.

Burt had already faced the killer, and Greg didn't know enough about Burt's condition to know if his friend would live or not.

And Lisa was the killer's next target.

At the moment, however, Lisa appeared to be safe. Every once in a while a police cruiser drove by and slowed, causing Greg's heart to beat faster. So far, the police hadn't seemed too interested in a family-type van.

Soon, people would start returning home from church. Then he'd need to take off.

It was time to act. Maybe he could park on the street behind Lisa's car for just ten minutes, dash up her stairs, knock, spew the necessary words and then take off before the undercover officer had time to realize what was going on.

He should have called her on the phone from Valentine. But he wanted to see for himself that she was safe. And he knew that, in person, he'd be more convincing. Maybe, like Burt, he'd wanted to see her face when he told her the truth, the whole devastating truth.

If it kept her alive, this wild and reckless detour was well worth it.

He checked his watch again. Ten-fifteen. Fifteen more minutes, then he was going to do something.

"Daddy, I'm hungry."

"Did you look in the sack?"

"I don't like anything in there."

Funny, last night at the convenience store in Ransome she'd liked everything they'd purchased.

The door of Lisa's apartment opened. A woman stepped out. She didn't look like a cop. In fact, she looked a lot like Lisa. But she wasn't. She didn't walk like Lisa, or hold her head like Lisa and at second glance, she was a bit taller. She pulled her coat, an expensive one, around her, and then slowly went down the stairs while talking on the telephone. She didn't look happy. After a moment, she cleared the snow off a front porch bench and settled in front of Lisa's landlord's front door.

Greg started the car. He was heading for the alley. He and Amber would come from the back, head up the stairs, warn Lisa and be gone before Lisa's friend, or whatever, knew what was happening.

"Daddy, what are we doing now?"

"We're going to visit your teacher."

"Can I come with you?"

"Of course, I wouldn't go anywhere without you."

She crossed her arms, looking too much like a mature female, and huffed, "Good."

He drove around the block, parked on the next street, thinking the whole way that it would serve him right if he got busted.

His watch said ten-thirty. He still had an hour before the church crowd hit the streets.

Amber was more than ready to get out of the van. She had the seat belt off and the door open before he made it around to the passenger door. Furtively, he looked up and down the street and then at the houses. Nothing looked amiss.

With Amber's hand tight in his, he cut across a lawn and went between two houses. He had to drag Amber up a slight slope before reaching the edge of Lisa's backyard. That's when he got a good look at the snow in Lisa's backyard.

Somebody had the same idea as he did. There were already prints in the newly fallen snow. Only they came from the side instead of behind the house.

It didn't matter what direction they came from.

They were fresh.

They led right to the stairs up to Lisa's apartment.

Greg grabbed Amber by the arm and ran around the house. She was so surprised she only managed a "What, Daddy, what?" before they rounded the corner and the woman on the front porch squeaked and dropped her phone.

"Are you a cop?" Greg yelled, skidding to a stop. "You gotta help. Someone's up there with Lisa."

The woman stood, quickly maneuvering so she was behind the bench. "I'm not a cop. I'm Lisa's sister. Alex Cooke, there are police officers everywhere. A cruiser drives by every ten minutes. I suggest—"

He was getting tired of people telling him to turn himself in.

Plus, he didn't have time for this. "I suggest," he said quickly, "that you notice that I'm not moving toward you, I'm not holding a gun on you and I'm trying to help your sister. I'm telling you to take my daughter and get to your car and move!

Call the police! Get them here! Whoever killed my wife is up in the apartment with Lisa. I'm going up there now."

"Why should I believe you?" Tamara snarled.

Before Greg could answer, they heard the sound of a gunshot.

For the last year, he'd done nothing but flee from trouble. Now he was running full throttle toward it. Behind him he could hear Amber screaming and crying Daddy over and over. As he took the stairs two at a time, slipping on the ice but with a sure enough grip to pull himself upward, he prayed that Lisa's sister—with his daughter in tow—was hurrying toward her car. He also hoped she was multitasking enough to dial 911 on her cell phone.

Lisa's door was half open. He pushed it the rest of the way and flew in.

The smell of gunpowder permeated the room. It managed to overpower the cold. Greg paused once he stepped over the threshold and into Lisa's living room. He'd expected noise—lots of it. But the apartment was amazingly quiet.

Actually, Lisa lived in a fugitive's dream home. He could see everything. To the left was her bedroom. To the right was the kitchen.

"Alex Cooke, how nice of you to drop in."

The man stood by a small kitchen table. He wore a familiar-looking red-and-black-checkered jacket. The jeans were non-descript. The boots were brown, scruffed and identical to Greg's. The blue knit hat was pushed far enough back on the man's forehead to prove to anyone who got close enough—or whoever really knew Alex Cooke—that they were not one and the same.

From a distance, though, or maybe even on a black-and-white surveillance camera, the resemblance was uncanny.

Thanks to makeup.

"I thought he was you," Lisa said. She sat at the table, hands folded in front of her like a schoolgirl. Her face was pale. No surprise. For an innocent, she was amazingly calm.

Christopher Engstrom had a gun pointed at her head.

"This couldn't possibly be better," the man grinned. "I'll get to see your face when I kill your girlfriend."

"She's not my girlfriend." Greg gripped the door. He could probably slip outside; maybe Engstrom would give chase. "She's my daughter's teacher. Let her go."

Or maybe Engstrom wouldn't give chase.

"Right," Engstrom said. "You're here because she's a friend. You've always been *such* a Boy Scout."

The sarcasm oozed. His tone implied that Greg was anything but a Boy Scout. Engstrom insinuated that Greg cared for Lisa.

He was right.

"What's really great about this is that I can kill Lisa and slip away. And guess who will get blamed?"

"Not me," Greg said. "When the gun went off, I was on the front porch talking to Lisa's sister."

Engstrom snarled at Lisa. "Why did you have to fight? Just like Rachel."

Greg's eyes followed Lisa's to a hole in the ceiling.

"I thought he was you," Lisa told Greg again. "Then, once I realized my mistake, I tried to get past him."

Engstrom said, "It's your fault Rachel is dead. She should have been with me in the first place. I loved her more than you did."

Time. If Greg could just buy enough time, the cops might arrive, might bust in here. No, they wouldn't need to bust, the door was wide open. The cold was like a fourth person in the room. There had to be something Greg could do, say...

"If you loved her," Greg said, "why'd you kill her?"

"I didn't," Engstrom insisted. "You did. It's your fault. I was offering her everything you offered her and more. I made sure I had money, like you did. And after the bank robbery, you were supposed to be out of the picture. Then you escaped. If you hadn't escaped, she'd still be alive."

He had started to shake. The gun edged close to Lisa's brow. Greg stopped talking. Who knew what really motivated this man? Taking a step back, Greg tried to regroup, tried to think of what to do, but Lisa's sister did it for him. He'd been concentrating so much on Engstrom that he hadn't heard the woman coming up the stairs.

With a baseball bat, no less.

She handed it to him. He grabbed it, turned and ran toward Engstrom. It was only four steps.

It was all happening so fast. Engstrom almost looked like he was laughing, but at least the gun was no longer pointed at Lisa.

It was pointed at Greg.

Engstrom pulled the trigger.

As Greg fell, as blood started to cover his eyes and fill his mouth, through a slit he saw Lisa whack Engstrom over the head with a Bible.

His last thought, before passing out, was that he hadn't thought she owned one.

For more than an hour after Greg was brought to the emergency room, no one knew if he'd live or not. The crowd who wanted to know grew by the minute. At one time there were more than thirty people gathered to see how Alex was doing. Many of them, like the softball team and the church members, only stayed long enough to pray. Some of Alex's coworkers showed up, too. Vince Frenci held Lisa's hand and even bowed his head in prayer, though Lisa noticed that he didn't close his eyes.

She hadn't closed hers, either.

She was afraid she'd miss something, like the doctor looking around to give her an update to and not seeing her. The media, thanks to Jake, couldn't get past the front doors.

All but the most determined were turned away.

When Lisa's father lay dying, only her sisters and her mother were there. Lisa couldn't remember if they'd said a prayer. All she remembered was the quiet.

Finally, a nurse came and said a doctor would be with them in a minute. Then a doctor motioned her over. Lisa took two steps toward the swinging doors that separated the rooms from the public and bumped into Jake.

"Lisa, I should go in first. I—"

"I had a gun pointed at my head for five minutes and I'm still sane. I deserve to go in."

The minister nodded. "She's right. And I need to be there for support also."

The doctor shook his head and said, "Sheriff, I'm only allowed by law to speak with you. The minister is probably fine if you want to bring in one guest. But if you want to know who he's asking for, besides his daughter, it's the lady."

In the end, all three entered the room. Machines beeped a continual reminder that all was not well. An IV stood like a sentry by Alex's left side. Gauze made the man look vulnerable, but his eyes, his brown eyes were alert.

"Five more minutes," Jake mourned. "Five more minutes and we'd have been there."

"Five more minutes and Lisa would be dead," Alex groused.

"I was holding my own," she protested, moving to the only chair, scooting it as close to him as the IV would allow. "I saved you, didn't I?"

He grinned weakly. "I didn't even know you owned a Bible."

It was the preacher who answered, "She doesn't. I was so

tired when I finally left there on Friday night that I forgot to take it with me. Lisa, consider that Bible yours."

"And the word shall set you free," Alex muttered.

"Not in Engstrom's case," Jake said. "That Bible's evidence right now and Engstrom is looking at a life sentence."

Lisa knew a little bit too much about the law, thanks to Tamara. "Unfortunately, insanity just might work in his case."

"He's still claiming that Rachel's death is Alex's fault," Jake said. "Down at the station, they can't get him to shut up. I think he thinks the more he talks, the more we'll believe him."

Alex closed his eyes.

"Amber's fine," Lisa said softly. "My sister took her over to Mrs. Griffin's. Tamara's staying with her. I think they bonded. As soon as you feel up to it, you need to call Amber. We promised her you would."

"How did you know?" Alex asked, looking at Jake.

"Your friend Burt came out of his coma this morning. He hollered until the nurse called the police. I guess he repeated Christopher Engstrom's name and some librarian's name often enough to make one of the officers take notice. He went to see the librarian."

"Shelly Moser?" Alex asked.

"That's the name. I guess Shelly Moser stumbled across a book about bank robberies, checked out just a year ago, by Christopher Engstrom. She told Burt. He went looking for Christopher Engstrom."

"A library book," Alex said in wonder. "A library book finally pointed at Christopher Engstrom."

Jake nodded. "Unfortunately, it looks like Christopher Engstrom was already looking for Burt.

"So," Alex said, looking at Jake, "exactly what charges will I face now that Christopher Engstrom has been arrested?"

"Embezzlement, grand theft, fraud—"

Lisa took Alex's hand. "Cops always go for the worst-case scenario. You concentrate on getting better. I know that bullet only grazed your head, but it scared me to death. They'll release you in the morning. Jake's already arranged for Amber to stay with me starting tomorrow. You have nothing to worry about."

He started to shake his head, but stopped, turning pale enough to show Lisa what pain looked like.

A nurse stepped in at that moment. "Your five minutes were up fifteen minutes ago," she said. "I'm tougher than the doc. The rules are one visitor."

The sheriff and the minister looked at each other and shrugged. Miles Pynchon left. The sheriff walked toward the curtain. The nurse disappeared, and the sheriff hesitated. "You still have to face charges. You know that."

Alex nodded and said, "I know, and I want to know what Engstrom is saying. Lisa deserves to hear, too."

"I'll make it quick then," Jake said. "In a nutshell, Christopher Engstrom became fixated on your late wife back when his mother cleaned her family's house. Rachel must have been in grade school. Then he worked at the high school while she attended there and even helped with the drama club."

Jake shook his head. "I'm not sure what he was up to the years after Rachel graduated from high school, but it looks like he went to every community theater production Rachel was in. Then he attended your high school reunion two years ago. Apparently, once he saw Rachel and you together, he lost it."

"And because he lost it, I lost it," Alex muttered.

"You're a modern-day Job," Jake agreed. "But like Job, you have a lot to live for. There's a little girl just dying to hear that her daddy is all right. And there's a big girl in here holding your hand."

Alex closed his eyes. His hand had been relaxed in Lisa's grip. Now his fingers moved until he was holding on tight, as if he'd never let go. "Go on," he said. "I know there's more."

"Just a bit," Jake agreed. "Engstrom robbed your bank both to get money and to frame you. The bank robbery went perfectly, according to him. Then, when he showed up at your house looking a bit like you and expecting Rachel to pack a bag and hop in the car, his luck changed. Rachel refused to go with him, and he was surprised. He truly expected her to be glad to see him."

Jake's voice changed, going from pure cop to pure friend. "You need to know this. He didn't mean to kill her. He got her from the house and into his car. They made it all the way to Yudan, her fighting all the way. He only meant to use the gun to subdue her. When it discharged and she died, he went even crazier. He blamed you. And when the cops seemed to stop looking for you, he finally allowed Rachel's body to surface, hoping once again to frame you."

"Allowed the body to be found," Alex said gruffly. "I just can't imagine the way this man's mind works."

"It doesn't work," Lisa stated. "He's sick."

"So sick," Jake agreed, "that when Rachel died, he tried to save her, the only way he knew how."

"And how was that?" Alex asked.

"You don't want to know," Jake answered.

"I do want to know!" Alex said.

Jake glanced at Lisa. Alex did, too. Her fingers digging into the side of his arm. "Maybe we should to this later."

"No," Lisa said. "I'm here as long as you need me."

"Let's just say, his theater background came in handy. He knew how to use makeup, lacquer and salt as a mixture. Then—" Jake slowed "—the plastic he covered her with helped a lot."

Lisa was amazed by what Alex had gone through and survived. She let go of his arm and twined her fingers with his before saying softly, "Christopher Engstrom almost succeeded in ruining your life a second time. But he didn't. You should see the people who showed up in the waiting room, all hoping to hear that you were going to be okay. You should have heard the prayers."

Alex's eyes were closing. His grip loosened as whatever drugs they'd given him took effect. Still, he managed to smile. "Engstrom didn't count on me showing up during the final act."

The headaches would go away, the doctor had promised. It had been a month, and Alex no longer believed the man. Plus, not all headaches were of the migraine variety. Most of Alex's headaches were either due to the media attention or the cops returning with, just a few more questions…

For the last month, Alex spent more time at the police station or the courthouse than he did at home. As for the media, having them show up on the day he and Amy finally got to visit Rachel's grave was inexcusable. On that day, the cops had earned his respect. He wasn't quite sure he had theirs, yet, but they'd certainly impressed him.

After doing the regular Sunday morning meet and greet, he finally settled into his favorite pew. He placed his Bible beside him, and out of habit more than anything, looked around.

Everyone and everything was in their place. Upfront, Miles Pynchon was storing a glass of water for the sermon. One of the elders was passing out bulletins. Children were running toward classes while parents chanted, *Walk*.

Amy had been the first to show up for Miss Magee's class.

She had plenty to tell her teacher. First and foremost was that over the Christmas holiday her daddy was letting her spend the night at Tiffany's. Next, Daddy would probably be getting a new job. She'd end with the fact that her daddy's friend Burt was getting out of the hospital and coming for a visit.

Alex and Burt still had some issues to deal with. Alex's ordeal was far from over. He still faced charges that could land him in jail, but a month ago he'd been wanted for two counts of murder. What he was wanted for now seemed almost benign.

"Mind if I sit here?"

He'd mind if she didn't. In the month since Engstrom's arrest, Alex had taken Lisa out to dinner a dozen times. A couple of times, he'd even gotten a sitter. Then, as a family, they'd gone bowling, roller skating and to the movies.

She'd attended church with him once.

Now here she was of her own accord.

He moved his Bible and scooted over, whispering, "I'm glad you're here."

"Me, too. By the way, I saw you talking to Perry…"

He almost laughed. It was good to deal with the everyday give-and-take of a fledgling friendship.

"I asked him if he'd meet me for lunch one day this week. I figured he could use a friend."

"You're kidd— No, I guess you're not. Reaching out to someone like Perry is exactly what I am learning to expect from you." She'd curled her red hair, something she didn't do too often. She wore an emerald-green dress he hadn't seen before. She'd gone out of her way to dress up, *for him.*

She nestled in beside him, so close he could smell her perfume and feel the heat of her body. She placed her Bible, the one the preacher had given her, in her lap.

"I've been trying to read this," she said. "It's not making a lot of sense yet."

"Are you here because you want it to make sense?"

She was quiet for a minute. "I'm here because *you* make sense."

Not only did he *not* know how to answer that, but he was also afraid to answer, so he waited.

"Jake compared you to Job. I've been reading about him. I can't even imagine a God who would test someone like that. Yet, I know how you've been tested and here you are, attending church, moving forward, forgiving Perry. It's amazing."

He didn't feel amazing. He still felt exhausted. Well, he'd felt exhausted until Lisa showed up and sat down beside him.

"I spoke with the minister last night," Lisa continued. "He told me that the real Greg Bond isn't pressing charges."

Alex winced. He still hadn't wrapped his mind around Greg's generosity concerning Alex's debt. Greg Bond, the missionary in Africa, refused to press charges and claimed that he was spending time and money overseas to save souls and that, in a roundabout way, without him even knowing, God was using his resources in the States to do the same thing.

"Amazing," Lisa said.

Alex could only agree.

"I figure you guys knew something I don't, and teachers make excellent students."

She didn't look like a student. She didn't look like a teacher. She looked… She looked like the answer to a prayer he hadn't deserved to utter.

Then, just as she had in the emergency room, she reached over and took his hand.

Upfront, a man had stepped behind the podium for the opening prayer. "Let's give thanks to God," he said.

Alex squeezed Lisa's hand. Giving thanks didn't seem quite enough, but that's what he intended to do.

His headache was gone; his life was beginning again.

He leaned over and kissed Lisa on the cheek.

Amen.

* * * * *

Dear Reader,

Where do story ideas come from? Well, for *Fugitive Family*, the story came to me while I was waiting in a long line at my bank. I happened to look up at the mirror they had mounted to the ceiling. *Hmmm, I've gained a bit of weight. Hmmm, I thought my hair was a bit fluffier than that. Hmmm, why did I leave the house in this outfit?* By the time I finished humming, I wondered if the reflection was really me.

It was, of course, and that moment in time gave birth to a book.

Sometimes the book belongs to the hero; sometimes it belongs to the heroine. The book belongs to Alex. I truly enjoyed watching him go from a detached father to a hands-on father. Lisa was fun, too. She was such an innocent. Believe me, there are innocents out there. No wonder Alex was drawn to her.

Thank you so much for reading Alex and Lisa's story. I love hearing from my readers. Please visit my blog; http://ladiesofsuspense.blogspot.com.

You may also contact me at www.pamelakeyetracy.com or at Pamela Tracy, c/o Steeple Hill Books, 233 Broadway, Suite 1001, New York, NY 10279.

Blessings,

Pamela Tracy

QUESTIONS FOR DISCUSSION

1. We are taught to trust the authorities—think innocent until proven guilty. So were Alex's actions early on, when he walked out of the police station, took Amber and ran, justified?

2. How and why did his years in the foster-care system affect Alex's marriage to Rachel? How did it affect him as a father to Amy? How do you think it will affect his relationship with Lisa?

3. From the beginning, Burt urged Alex to be seen, get alibis, fit in. Was this good advice?

4. The church's softball team is a place of camaraderie and fun. What, outside of regular church services, are you favorite activities with your church friends? Does that activity open the door for spiritual growth?

5. Alex basically stole Greg Bond's identity and his money. After Alex became a Christian, how did his thoughts change concerning this crime? Do you understand his actions when it came to maintaining the false identity? Why or why not?

6. When did Alex fall in love with Lisa? When did Lisa fall in love with Alex? If there hadn't been a relationship brewing just under the surface, how might the story have ended?

7. Christopher Engstrom became fixated on Rachel. He went to extremes. Now that he's in jail, what should his punishment be?

8. The real Greg Bond is a missionary in Africa. What motivates him to forgive and forget Alex's debt? What impression does this make on Lisa?

9. Alex and Perry are going to meet and have a talk. How do you think Alex can best influence Perry?

10. Lisa is starting to show an interest in the Bible. Imagine someone who has never been introduced to the Word. What steps should Alex take to help her gain a basic understanding, especially considering that she'd starting with Job?

A thrilling romance between a British nurse and
an American cowboy on the African plains.

Turn the page for a sneak preview of
THE MAVERICK'S BRIDE
by Catherine Palmer.
Available September 2009
from Love Inspired® Historical.

Adam hoisted himself onto the balcony, swinging one leg at a time over the rail. He hoped he hadn't been spotted by a compound guard.

But the sight of Emma Pickering peering out from behind the curtain put his concerns to rest. He had done the right thing.

"Good morning, Miss Pickering." He leaned against the white window frame.

"Mr. King." She was almost breathless. "I cannot speak with you."

"But I need to talk. Mind if I come inside?"

"Indeed, sir, you may not take another step! Are you mad?"

He couldn't hold back a grin. "No more than most. I figure anyone who would leave home and travel all the way to Africa has to be a little off-kilter."

"You refer to me, I suppose? I'll have you know I'm here for a very good reason."

"Railway inspection, is it? Or nursing?"

Emma looked even better than he had thought she might—and he had thought about her a lot.

"Speaking of nursing," he ventured.

"Mr. King, I have already told you I'm unavailable. Now please let yourself down by that…that rope thing, and—"

"My lasso?"

"You must go down again, sir. This is unseemly."

Emma was edgy this morning. Almost frightened. Different from the bold young woman he had met yesterday.

He couldn't let that concern him. Last night after he left the consulate, he had made up his mind to keep things strictly business with Emma Pickering.

"I'll leave after I've had my say," he told her. "This is important."

"Speak quickly, sir. My father must not find you here."

"With all due respect, Emma, do you think I'm concerned about what your father thinks?"

"You may not care, but I do. What do you want from me?"

"I need a nurse."

"A nurse? Are you ill?"

"Not for me. I have a friend—at my ranch."

Her eyes deepened in concern as she let the curtain drop a little. "What sort of illness does your friend have? Can you describe it?"

Adam looked away. How could he explain the situation without scaring her off?

"It's not an illness. It's more like…"

Searching for the right words, he turned back to Emma. But at the first full sight of her face, he reached through the open window and pulled the curtain out of her hands.

"Emma, what happened to you?" He caught her arm and drew her toward him. "Who did this?"

She raised her hand in a vain effort to cover her cheek and eye. "It's nothing," she protested, trying to back away. "Please, Mr. King, you must not…"

Even as she tried to speak, he stepped through the balcony

door and gathered her into his arms. Brushing back the hair from her cheek, he noted the swelling and the darkening stain around it.

"Emma," he growled. "Who did this to you?"

She fell motionless, silent in his embrace. No wonder she had shied like a scared colt. She hadn't wanted him to know.

Torn with dismay that anyone would ever harm this beautiful woman, he felt an irresistible urge to kiss her.

"Emma, you have to tell me…." Realization flooded through him. A pompous, nattily dressed English railroad tycoon had struck his own daughter.

"Leave me, I beg you. You have no place here."

"Emma, wait. Listen to me." Adam caught her wrists and pulled her back toward him. He'd never been a man to think things through too carefully. He did what felt right.

"I want you to come with me," he told her. "I need your help. Let's go right now. Emma, I'll take care of you."

"I don't need anyone to take care of me," she shot back. "God is watching over me."

"Emma!" Both turned toward the open door where Emma's sister stood, eyes wide.

"Emma, go with him!" Cissy crossed the room toward them. "Run away with him, Emma. It's your chance to escape—to become a nurse, as you've always wanted. You'll be safe at last, and you can have your dream."

Emma turned back to Adam.

"Come on," he urged her. "Let's get moving."

* * * * *

*Will Emma run away with Adam and finally
realize her dreams of becoming a nurse?
Find out in THE MAVERICK'S BRIDE,
available in September 2009 only from
Love Inspired® Historical.*

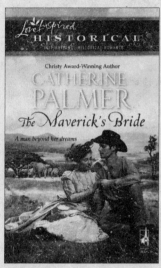

REQUEST YOUR FREE BOOKS!

2 FREE RIVETING INSPIRATIONAL NOVELS
PLUS 2 FREE MYSTERY GIFTS

Love Inspired®
SUSPENSE

YES! Please send me 2 FREE Love Inspired® Suspense novels and my 2 FREE mystery gifts (gifts are worth about $10). After receiving them, if I don't wish to receive any more books, I can return the shipping statement marked "cancel". If I don't cancel, I will receive 4 brand-new novels every month and be billed just $4.24 per book in the U.S. or $4.74 per book in Canada. That's a savings of over 20% off the cover price. It's quite a bargain! Shipping and handling is just 50¢ per book.* I understand that accepting the 2 free books and gifts places me under no obligation to buy anything. I can always return a shipment and cancel at any time. Even if I never buy another book, the two free books and gifts are mine to keep forever.

123 IDN EYM2   323 IDN EYNE

Name	(PLEASE PRINT)	
Address		Apt. #
City	State/Prov.	Zip/Postal Code

Signature (if under 18, a parent or guardian must sign)

Mail to Steeple Hill Reader Service:
IN U.S.A.: P.O. Box 1867, Buffalo, NY 14240-1867
IN CANADA: P.O. Box 609, Fort Erie, Ontario L2A 5X3

Not valid to current subscribers of Love Inspired Suspense books.

Want to try two free books from another series?
Call 1-800-873-8635 or visit www.morefreebooks.com

* Terms and prices subject to change without notice. Prices do not include applicable taxes. Sales tax applicable in N.Y. Canadian residents will be charged applicable provincial taxes and GST. Offer not valid in Quebec. This offer is limited to one order per household. All orders subject to approval. Credit or debit balances in a customer's account(s) may be offset by any other outstanding balance owed by or to the customer. Please allow 4 to 6 weeks for delivery. Offer available while quantities last.

LISUS09

Love Inspired®
SUSPENSE

TITLES AVAILABLE NEXT MONTH
Available September 8, 2009

FINAL EXPOSURE by Roxanne Rustand
Big Sky Secrets
Safety and serenity are what Jack Matthews seeks in
Lost Falls, Montana. But when Jack discovers that his
beautiful host, Erin Cole, is being stalked, how much will
Jack have to risk to keep her safe?

A SILENT FURY by Lynette Eason
One girl from the Palmetto Deaf School is dead, and another
has been taken. Detective Catelyn Clark will do anything to
save the kidnapped girl...even work with her ex, FBI agent
Joseph Santino.

RACE TO RESCUE by Dana Mentink
Her beloved brother is missing somewhere in the harsh
Arizona desert, but the police won't take Anita Teel's
fears seriously. Only one man will: Booker Scott, the
hardened rancher who broke her heart, and will have to risk
everything to help her now.

PROTECTOR'S HONOR by Kit Wilkinson
Why is someone trying to kill Tabitha Beaumont? That's
what NCIS agent Rory Farrell vows to find out. She needs
protection–Rory's protection–while Rory needs answers
Tabitha doesn't even realize she holds. Yet how can he find
the truth without betraying Tabitha's trust?

LISCNMBPA0809